VICTORIA LIN

'Reading these someone talkin simply pleasur much want to hear' ction of all – you very

Sunday Telegraph

'Maeve Binchy reads the fantasies and lives of others with devastating clarity. Her distinction is that her stories are dramatically credible'

Scotsman

'Each story is an absolute delight . . . All have a perceptive warmth and love of humanity . . . Maeve Binchy's story-telling art is exquisite. It is immensely readable'

East Anglian Daily Times

The book is left
behind with thanks
for some very happy
memories —
love Anna

May 1989

Maeve Binchy was born in Dublin, and went to school at the Holy Child Convent in Killiney. She took a history degree at UCD and taught in various girls' schools, writing travel articles in the long summer holidays. In 1969 she joined the *Irish Times*. For the last eight years she has been based in London and writes humorous columns from all over the world. The Peacock Theatre in Dublin was the scene of her two stage plays, *End of Term* and *Half Promised Land*, and her television play, *Deeply Regretted By*, won two Jacobs Awards and the Best Script Award at the Prague Film Festival. She is the author of two other volumes of short stories, *Central Line* and *Dublin 4* and of the bestselling novel, *Light A Penny Candle*. Maeve Binchy is married to the writer and broadcaster Gordon Snell.

Victoria Line

Maeve Binchy

CORONET BOOKS
Hodder and Stoughton

To Gordon with all my love

Copyright © 1978, 1979, 1980, 1982 by Maeve Binchy

Warren Street was first published as *The Dressmaker's Dilemma* in *Woman's Own*, June 1979; *Central* and *Pimlico* were first published in the *Irish Times*, 1979.

Victoria Line was first published in Great Britain in 1983 by Quartet Books and Ward River Press Limited. It appeared as part of a hardback edition entitled *London Transports* published by Century Ltd in 1983.

Coronet edition 1984.

British Library C.I.P.

Binchy, Maeve
 Victoria Line
 I. Title
 823'.914[F]   PR6052.17728

ISBN 0–340–34002–9

Printed and bound in Great Britain for Hodder and Stoughton Paperbacks, a division of Hodder and Stoughton Ltd., Mill Road, Dunton Green, Sevenoaks, Kent (Editorial Office: 47 Bedford Square, London, WC1 3DP) by Cox & Wyman Ltd., Reading

Contents

Tottenham Hale	1
Seven Sisters	11
Finsbury Park	22
Highbury & Islington	31
King's Cross	41
Euston	64
Warren Street	77
Oxford Circus	86
Green Park	97
Victoria	109
Pimlico	119
Vauxhall	127
Stockwell	136
Brixton	146

To Gordon with all my love.

Tottenham Hale

Amy watched six taxis avoid her and go deliberately towards other people. Then she began to realize she was suffering from advanced paranoia and that she had better cut her losses and take the tube home. She was already so late and angry, that the lurching crowded journey couldn't make her much worse. And there was the danger that if she stood much longer on the side of the street being ignored by rush hour taxi drivers she might lose her small remaining ration of sanity. And she needed to hold on to what she had for tonight.

Tonight Ed's sister and her husband were coming to dinner. Tonight, for the first time, she would meet the Big Mama figure in Ed's American family, the one they all bowed to, the one Ed had practically written to for permission to marry Amy. At the time Amy had thought it funny; she had even suggested that her dental reports and photostats of her G.C.E. certificates be sent to New York. But three years later, after a period of watching Ed write his monthly letter to his big sister Bella, she found it less funny. She was never shown these letters and in pique she had opened one before posting it. It was an infantile report on how their life had been progressing since last month: childish details about the floor covering they had bought for the kitchen, aspirations that Ed's salary would be reviewed and upped. Praise for a new dress that Amy had bought, minutiae about a picnic they had had with another couple. It had made Amy uneasy, because it had made Ed seem retarded. It was the kind of letter that a mother might expect from a small son who had gone off to summer camp, not something that a sister in far away America should need or want.

Ed had been euphoric about the visit. It had been planned for over three months. Bella and her husband Blair were coming to London for three days as part of a European tour. They would arrive in the morning; they did not want to be met, they preferred to recover from their jet lag alone in the privacy of a good hotel with a comfortable bedroom and bathroom. Fully refreshed, at seven p.m. they would come and see their beloved Ed and welcome their new sister Amy to the family. Next day there would be a tour to Windsor and an evening at the theatre, with a dinner for the four of them; and on the Saturday morning, Amy might kindly take her new sister Bella shopping, and point out the best places, introduce her to the heads of departments in the better stores. They would have a super girly lunch, and then Bella and Blair would fly out of their lives to Paris.

Normally, on any ordinary Thursday, Amy came home from Harley Street, where she worked as a doctor's receptionist, took off her shoes, put on her slippers, unpacked her shopping, organized a meal, lit the fire and then Ed would arrive home. Their evenings had begun to have a regular pattern. Ed came home tense and tired. Little by little, in front of the fire, he would unwind; little by little he relaxed his grip on the file of papers he had brought back from the office. He would have a sherry, his face would lose its lines; and then he would agree really that there was no point in trying to do too much work in the evening.

With a glass of wine, he would say that the Labourer was worthy of his Hire, and he would expand about people being entitled to their leisure. And afterwards, he would carve away happily at the table he was making, or watch television, or do the crossword with Amy;

and she realized happily that she was essential to him, because only her kind of understanding could make him uncoil and regard his life as a happy, unworrying thing.

That was all before the threatened visit of Bella.

For three months now, he hadn't been able to relax. No matter how many blandishments and encouragements Amy put in his way, he seemed stressed and anxious. He was anxious on all fronts: Bella would think it strange that he hadn't moved out of sales into middle management before this; he must show Bella what the structure of the company was, he must prove to her that he had done as much home work and extra work as he could possibly do. Every night his briefcase bulged with sheets of incomprehensible figures. But this wasn't all. He couldn't even concentrate on the office work, he would jump up and spot some defect in the house.

'Heavens, Amy, that curtain rail is missing three hooks, can you fix it darling? Please.'

Sometimes he said: 'Before Bella comes', sometimes he didn't. He didn't even need to, really. Amy knew.

The phone mouthpiece was dirty, the bath-mat had got worn-looking, the window boxes needed repainting, the carving dish had one of its feet twisted the wrong way, the ice trays in the refrigerator were both cracked.

About a dozen times, Amy had reacted and explained that Bella was not coming on a mission of inspection; she hadn't flown the Atlantic to check the curtains, the telephone or the ice trays, she had come to see Ed. But his face just became more worried and he said that he would like things to be right.

So right was everything, that Amy was almost a nervous wreck. The house had been polished within an inch of its life. A magnificent casserole was waiting to be reheated, good wine had been chosen, the table had been set before she left the house that morning. If Bella were to go through the house with a fleet of police specially trained in house-searches, nothing damaging could be revealed. No hidden mounds of rubbish or unsorted paraphernalia in any cupboard. If Bella decided to pull back the sitting-room carpet and examine the underlay she would not be able to find fault.

Magazines and newspapers praising the excellence of this part of North London had been laid around strategically, so that Bella's gaze could be diverted to them should she disapprove of the suburb where Ed and Amy lived. They had even alerted one set of neighbours of the possibility that they might take Bella and Blair over for a drink if they wanted to say 'Hi' to some local people.

Amy had asked for the afternoon off, and she had spent it at the beautician's. She had suggested it herself and Ed's kind, worried face had lit up.

'It's not that you don't look lovely already, Amy,' he had said, afraid to offend her. 'It's just that ... well, you know, I told Bella you were so groomed, and you know the photographs we send ... well, we always send ones that make us look good.'

Bella was no oil painting, Amy often thought in rage. She was downright plain; she was tall and rather severe. Her clothes in the pictures that Ed had shown her – photographs taken some years back – had been simple and neat with no concession to fashion. Why, then, had Ed spent nights deliberating over Amy's wardrobe and planning what she should wear? Bella was a teacher, and Blair had some unspecified job in the same school, administration Ed thought, but he didn't really give it any time. None of the family gave Blair any time, he was good to Bella as a consort. He was mute and supportive. That was all that was needed. Bella's four younger brothers owed her everything. They would never have gone through school if she hadn't urged them; they wouldn't have got good jobs, and married

4

suitable women without her wise influence; they would be nothings, hopeless orphans, rudderless, had not Bella persuaded the authorities to let her play Mama at the age of fifteen. Ed had only been five then, he couldn't even remember the mother and father who went into a lake in a drunken motor-accident.

Sometimes Amy wondered about the other sisters-in-law. Wasn't it odd that the sons had all gone so far afield from beloved Bella? There was a brother who had gone to California – that was about as far as you could get from New York State; and one was in Vancouver, and one in Mexico, and Ed was in London. Amy suspected that her three sisters-in-law and she would get along famously. She felt sure they were united in a common hatred of Bella and what she was doing to their men.

But no hint of this escaped in any of the family letters, all of which seemed to be full of Bella. When she had been in bed for three weeks with influenza, letters posted in San José, Vancouver and Mexico City had crashed on to the mat in Tottenham Hale giving the latest bulletins. The three brothers had written to Ed in terms of congratulation and encouragement once the visit of Bella to England had been announced. Bella's own letters were short and terse, and offered little news of her own life, only praise or enquiry about the life of the recipient. The more Amy thought about her, the more she became convinced that Bella was mad.

Now, beautifully coiffed, elegantly made-up, manicured, massaged at a cost which left her seething with rage, Amy stood on the platform waiting for the train to take her home to meet this monster. She got a couple of admiring looks which pleased her; a student pinched her bottom hard, which hurt her and annoyed her; but with confidence gained from parting with the huge sum of money to the beauty salon she said clearly and loudly, 'Please don't do that again,' and everybody looked at the student who went scarlet and got out at the next station. Two men congratulated her and she felt pleased that she was becoming mature.

She worked out that she would have two hours at home before the dreaded Bella arrived. That would be time to do the final fixing of the meal, have a bath and dress. Ed had taken the afternoon off and he was going to have arranged fresh flowers and done any last minute things.

'Won't she think it strange that you took time off work to do housework?' asked Amy.

'If she doesn't ask, we mightn't have to tell her,' he said, giggling like a schoolboy.

Amy told herself firmly that she was not a criminal, she hadn't kidnapped Ed, she had loved him and married him. She looked after him well by any standards, she encouraged him when he felt down but she didn't push him on to impossible heights. This appalling Bella couldn't fault her on her performance, surely? And if that was all true, which it undoubtedly was, then why did she feel so apprehensive? The train gave a great lurch which flung all those still standing into each other's arms. Carefully, they disentangled themselves, with little laughs and apologies; and it was a few moments before they realized that the train had actually stopped and they were not at a station.

'That's all we need,' said a florid-looking man with a briefcase. 'Told the wife I'd be home early, and now we're going to be stuck here all night.'

'Surely not?' asked a woman who looked tired and miserable. She was carrying a heavy bag of shopping. 'There'll be nobody to let the children in,' she added in a worried tone.

Amy began to realize the situation. Every minute here was a minute less in the elaborate count-down for Bella's arrival. If they were fifteen minutes delayed, then she might have to go without a bath. If they were half-an-hour delayed she might have to lose bath, and decorating the trifle. Her mind couldn't take in anything longer than half-an-hour's delay.

Very soon, a uniformed man came through the carriage assuring them that there was no danger, no crisis, but that there had been a fault which must be corrected, and that London Transport apologized infinitely but there would be a delay.

No, he didn't know how long the delay would be.

Yes, he could assure them that there would be no danger.

No, there was no possibility of another train running into them.

Yes, he understood that it was a great inconvenience.

No. There was no way of doing anything more quickly than it was already being done.

Yes, people would be electrocuted and die if they stepped out on to the rails.

'That would appear to be that,' said the florid man. He looked at Amy appreciatively. 'I suppose if we are to be marooned, I'm to be congratulated on finding such an elegant shipmate. I'm Gerald Brent by the way.'

'I'm Amy Baker,' said Amy smiling.

'Mrs Baker, would you care to have a drink with me?' said Gerald Brent. He took a bottle of wine out of his briefcase, a penknife with a corkscrew attachment, and the top of his vacuum flask.

Laughing, Amy accepted.

'I'll drink from the other side,' said Gerald.

The well-known patience and docility of Londoners was beginning to be evident around the compartment. People were settling down to read the *Standard* and the *News*; one man was even having a little sleep of sorts; the worried woman had taken out a woman's magazine and resigned herself.

'Wife's mother is coming to dinner,' said Gerald. 'Terrible old bat. I'm not sorry to miss her, really. Anyway, this wine is much too good for her. Have another drop.'

Amy took the refill and looked at him to see if he was joking.

7

'You don't really think we'll miss dinner, do you?' she asked.

'Bound to,' said Gerald. He explained what must have gone wrong on the line, how a safety mechanism had worked properly but it would mean that it now had to be rewound by hand. They would have to bring personnel into the tunnel to do this.

'Three or four hours, at least,' he said.

It just wasn't possible, that in the whole of London, one tube line should have a mechanical failure, and she should be on it. It was simply beyond belief that this should happen on this one day out of the thousand or so days she had been married to Ed. It was quite inconceivable that Bella, the big black shadow over all their lives, was going to become like a mushroom cloud of menace and disappointment ever more. Ed would never recover from it. The evening would be a shambles, he would run out into the street looking for her. He might believe that she had left him as some kind of protest about Bella. Amy felt a wave of nausea at the horror of her situation, her face whitened and she looked as if she was going to fall.

'Steady,' said Gerald. 'You mustn't rush that wine, it's very good, full bodied, rich. Here. Sit on this corner.' He moved her to the corner of someone's seat. A London mateyness had now begun to develop and people who would have travelled unspeaking for years became animated and friendly through shared disaster.

Amy told Gerald all about Bella: she told him about opening the letter, she told him that Bella had strong-armed all her brothers into a forced, humble, gratitude. As she told him, it became even clearer to her just how destructive Bella had been; and how in Vancouver, San José and Mexico City, as well as London, four normal men were working like nervous beavers to thank this woman for giving up her youth to rear them. While in fact, Amy realized suddenly, all that Bella had done was give full vent to normal maternal instincts, and got

8

in return praise from authorities and social services. From four brothers she had got a slavish devotion.

Amy and Gerald finished the bottle of wine. Gerald muttered an occasional word of encouragement, and, whenever Amy began to panic at the thought of the ruined evening, he offered reassurance.

'Nonsense, of course he'll know where you are. They'll have it on the local news.'

'Heavens, girl, relax, he'll ring the station, they'll tell him.'

'Good God, woman, Bella doesn't expect you to get a pickaxe and hack your way out!'

He told her that his wife thought he drank too much, and that he did. He had once had an affair with his secretary, which his wife had never discovered, or he *thought* she'd never discovered; but he hadn't enjoyed the intrigue side of it, so he ended it, and his secretary called him a chauvinist bastard in front of three senior partners in the firm. It had been very distressing.

Coffee and sandwiches were brought in from the next station and a real party atmosphere began to develop. There was even a sing-song and by the time they did get out at ten p.m. to the flashing of photographers' light-bulbs and the attention of waiting crowds, Amy was quite unconcerned about Bella and the whole, ruined evening.

It was with a shock that she recognized Bella's features on the platform. Peering into the crowds emerging from the train she looked worried, and anxious for Amy's safety. Behind her were a worried Ed and a worried Blair.

'There she is,' cried Bella running forward, arms out. 'Amy, my little sister, are you all right? Are you hurt? Have you been looked after? My poor Amy, what an ordeal, what a catastrophe, for you!' She released her to let Ed hug her, and Blair hold her in a manful, silent grip.

Gerald watched the scene, and raised his hat before going on his way with a quizzical laugh.

Together the four of them went out of the station. Bella didn't look severe or plain, she looked aglow with interest and concern. She had telephoned the police four times, she had made sure that the train had been in no danger, she had taken first aid things to the station just in case. But now how wonderful, it had all ended happily and they were on the way back to Ed and Amy's lovely home. It had looked so really beautiful when she had arrived, those really cute window boxes, and my, how nice Amy sure kept everything, when she had to telephone she noticed just how fresh and dainty the whole house was. Well now, they could all go back and have that really delicious-looking dinner that she knew was there.

Blair smiled a great stalwart and supportive smile. And Ed looked like a child who got the candy; and Amy wondered why she could have resented Bella coming, she was so pleased that she was here. And even more pleased that she liked everything. Now, Amy would really go out of her way to give her a good shopping trip on the Saturday morning. After all, the only important thing was to please Bella.

Seven Sisters

It was very odd that they should live in Seven Sisters, Pat thought for the hundredth time. It seemed too much of a coincidence that anyone who was giving a wife-swapping party, with uninhibited fun and carefree swinging for sophisticated couples, should just happen to live in a place with the group name of Seven Sisters. She had said so to Stuart as well.

'They have to live somewhere,' he said unhelpfully.

Pat had studied the *A to Z*.

'I don't really see why they call it Seven Sisters, it's more Hornsey really,' she complained.

'If they'd called it Hornsey you'd probably say that that was even more suggestive,' said Stuart mildly.

For two weeks before the party, Pat lived on a high level of anxiety. She examined her new set of underwear with a worried frown. It was red and black, the black bits were lace and, in one instance, a rosette. Again and again she tried them on in the bathroom and examined herself critically in the mirror. She looked so very white, and the dark colours made her look almost dead. She wondered whether this would fire all the men with lust, whether they would be driven insane by the combination of dead white skin, red silk and black lace, or whether one of the women would take her aside and advise her to use a fake tan lotion. The awful thing was that there was no one to ask. Even if she were to write to this appalling magazine where Stuart had first seen the article about wife-swapping and had replied to one of the box numbers, she still wouldn't get a reply in time.

Over and over she rehearsed what she would say: 'Hallo, *lovely* of you to ask us . . . what a super house.' No, she couldn't tell this terrifying harlot who owned the house in Seven Sisters that it was lovely of her to have invited Pat and Stuart, since Pat and Stuart had in their corrupt and pleasure-seeking way told the Seven Sisters lot that they wanted to come and take off their clothes and go to bed with a load of strangers. The more she reminded herself that this is what they had arranged to do, the more faint and foolish she felt.

Even though she tried to put it from her mind, she wondered if there would be time for any conversation before they got down to action. Would she find herself stark naked in a corner talking to some other naked housewife about the children's drama group or the new supermarket? Would Stuart stand naked laughing with new people about the tomatoes they grew in their allotment?

That was the kind of thing that happened at the ordinary parties they went to . . . tame little evenings where people kept their clothes on, and didn't mate with each other, and discussed how expensive the season tickets on the train had become, and how hard it was to find a doctor who could spend two minutes listening to you. Tame evenings, dull evenings. Getting in a rut, becoming old before their time, suburban even though they hadn't yet reached their middle-class suburbia, no excitement, nothing very different, nothing that made them gasp.

Two children, the national average, Stuart working in a bank . . .

God Almighty! – Suppose some of the bank's clients were at the party! It wasn't so ridiculous. People don't live beside their banks, some of them could easily live off the Seven Sisters Road. Had Stuart thought of that? She had better tell him, they could call it all off. It would be foolish to imperil his whole career . . . No. He must have thought of it and rejected it. He was utterly set on going to this party now. He would only think she was groping around for some excuse.

. . . nice little flat, no garden unfortunately, but then they went to the allotment at weekends. Children very strong and happy, love their school. Debbie in the school play again this term, and Danny hoping to be picked for the third team. Lots of friends at school always running in and out of the neighbours' houses too and playing in the adventure playground at the end of the road. Not an earth-shaking life, but a happy one . . . even the school Principal had said the other day . . .

Sweet God! – Suppose the school ever got to hear of this! How utterly shaming for Debbie and Danny to be branded the children of perverts, sexual freaks. They might even be asked to leave lest their family shame might taint the other children. Relax. How could the school hear of it, unless other parents, or indeed some of the staff, were there being uninhibited and swinging in sophisticated adult fun? . . . Yes, of course, if any-one was there, a conspiracy of silence would have to be maintained.

. . . anyway the school Principal had said that he had enormous admiration for the parents of today, since they made so many sacrifices for their children and were so supportive and aware of all their needs. But he felt sure that this effort was repaid in a thousand ways by the fact that they lived in a peaceful community, far away from the wars and tensions and differences that rend other countries.

Stuart had said that people who went to these parties were normal, ordinary, good, respectable citizens like everyone else. He said that all they were doing was trying to push forward the frontiers of pleasure. They were trying to add to the delights of normal sexual love between a married couple . . . and be less selfish about it . . . by offering to share that love with other married

13

couples. He had read, and he believed that there was a lot of truth in it, that this kind of generosity, this giving of your rights in your partner to other friends, was an act of love in itself. And, even more important in these treacherous days, it completely by-passed the need to be 'unfaithful' to the other partner – there would be no forbidden lovers, or illicit affairs. It would all be out in the open. It would be healthy and good.

Stuart talked about it with the enthusiasm he had when he first talked about his allotment. His eyes had that gleam that they once had when he had planned a life of self-sufficiency. The rest of London might starve, might poison itself with nuclear fall-out, but Stuart and Pat and Debbie and Danny would grow what they needed for survival on their little allotment, and, aha, who'd laugh then? Pat had asked mildly how Stuart would protect his runner beans and cabbages against twelve million starving Londoners, if they were the only family which had managed to be self-sufficient. Stuart had said it was a technicality.

The Saturday and Sunday gardening continued, it had lost its first flush of real excitement, but nowadays it brought them a gentle pleasure. Perhaps this would happen with wife-swapping too, Pat thought. Soon the heady excitement and flush of enthusiasm would pass, and they would settle into a weekly wife-swap happily and resignedly travelling to Seven Sisters, or Barking, or Rickmansworth, or Biggin Hill.

Stuart seemed so alarmingly calm about it all. This as much as anything disturbed Pat. She had asked him, did he think he should get new jockey-shorts.

'No, love, I've plenty up in the wardrobe,' he had said mystified.

'For the *party*,' she had hissed.

'Why should I need new jockey-shorts?' he had asked, as puzzled as if she had said he should buy a new transistor radio. 'I have nine pairs upstairs. I tell you, I have plenty.'

14

As the event drew nearer, Pat worried more about Stuart. Did he have no nerves, no feelings, that he could take it all so calmly . . . the fact that he had written to a box number and a woman with a voice like a circular saw had telephoned?

She had never given too much thought to their sex life. It had always seemed very pleasant and adequate, and she certainly didn't regard herself as frigid, not in the sense of the women's magazine articles on the topic. She couldn't remember saying that she had a headache, or that she didn't feel like it. There was, she supposed, a sort of sameness about it. But then, for heaven's sake, some things *are* the same. The taste of a bar of chocolate or a gin and lime is always the same. The sound of Beethoven's Fifth or Johnny Mathis is always the same. Why this great urge for something different?

Pat was hurt and puzzled. She had read about women who discovered that their meek and conventional husbands actually liked bondage or violent pornography . . . so perhaps she should feel relieved that Stuart had suggested only nice old middle-class wife-swapping. Still, Pat felt aggrieved. If she were prepared to live for the rest of their days with their life as it was now, saving for the house, going on a caravan holiday once a year, and making love comfortably in the darkness and privacy of their own room twice a week, then it was somehow ungrateful of Stuart not to feel the same about it.

Pat had an appointment with the hairdresser on the afternoon of the Terrible Day.

'Going somewhere nice?' asked the hairdresser in her bright, routine way.

'Eer . . . yes,' said Pat.

'Oh, to a function is it?' asked the hairdresser.

'Um. No, no. Not a function. Private house. Old friends, and new friends. A party. An ordinary party,' Pat screamed defensively.

The hairdresser shrugged.

'Very nice, I'm sure,' she said huffily.

15

The baby-sitter arrived on time. Pat had hoped that she might ring and say she couldn't come. That would mean the end of this ludicrous outing across London to copulate with strangers. The only tingles of excitement she felt were the ones which ran through her brain asking her if she were certifiably insane.

Debbie and Danny barely looked up from the television.

'Goodnight, Mum. Goodnight, Dad. Come in and see us when you get back.'

Pat's eyes filled with tears.

'Stuart love . . .' she began.

'Goodnight, you lot.' Stuart said firmly.

She had assumed that they would take the car and was startled when Stuart said that it was much simpler than driving to take the tube.

'Only one change,' he said. And to Pat the words seemed sinister and fraught with meaning. She wondered if he was saying that they would only swap with one couple when they got there. She felt nausea rise in her throat. Suppose it were like a dance in the tennis club years ago, when nobody asked you to dance and you ended up grateful for some awful person who eventually did suggest a shuffle around the floor. Could this happen tonight? Suppose some appalling, foul couple rejected by everyone else nodded encouragingly at them? Would they have to say yes? Did the house rules say that there was no opting out?

'Yes, but wouldn't it be nice to have the car coming home?' she asked.

'Mightn't feel like driving on the way back,' said Stuart succinctly.

Worn out with pleasure? Exhausted? Asleep on some strange other wife's bosom? Going home with someone else? Staying with the awful woman in Seven Sisters? What could he mean, he mightn't feel like driving? The whole nightmare was now quite frightening.

16

Why had she ever agreed to this wicked, and silly thing? Why had Stuart ever suggested it?

The tube came immediately, as trains always do when you are going to the dentist or a wife-swapping party. The stations flashed by. Stuart read the back of someone else's evening paper. Pat examined her face three times in her compact mirror.

'You look fine,' Stuart said to her when she got the compact out a fourth time.

'I suppose you're right. Anyway, it's not my face they'll be looking at,' she said resignedly.

'What? Oh. Oh yes,' said Stuart smiling supportively, and going back to reading the late football results.

'Do you think we'll take off our clothes immediately?' Pat asked wretchedly as they walked out of the station and towards the house.

'I don't know, I expect it depends on whether they have central heating,' Stuart said matter of factly.

Pat looked at him as if he were a total stranger.

'Did she give you any indication of how many people were going to be there?' Pat asked shrilly after another minute of walking. 'I mean, they're not very big houses. They can hardly have dozens.'

'No, she said just a few friends,' said Stuart. 'A few friends, she didn't say how many.'

'But we're not friends, we're sort of intruding on them in a way aren't we?' she begged. There were tears in her eyes. They were only one corner away from the house now. Right-turn that and they were in the road and there was no going back.

Stuart looked at her, moved by the tears he could hear in her voice.

'It'll be lovely, Pat dear. You'll love it. You're always a bit nervous at times like this.'

She looked at him, her eyes flashing.

'What do you mean at times like this? What "times like this" have there been before? When have we done

anything remotely like this. It's the only time like this
...' To her horror, she burst into tears.

Stuart looked very distressed. He tried to touch her,
to put his arm around her, but Pat pushed him away.

'No, stop saying it's all right, and that I'll love it. I'll
hate it. I'm not going. That's final.'

'Well why didn't you say this before? Why did you
wait until we're nearly there?' Stuart asked, his innocent, round face looking both foolish and puzzled at the
same time. 'I can't understand why you didn't say to me
that you thought it wasn't on, then we'd never have set
it all up. I thought you wanted to come too.'

Pat gave a snort into her tissues.

'You *said* it sounded an adventurous thing . . .' he
said.

Pat coughed loudly.

'You *said* we'd try it once and if we didn't like it we'd
have got it out of our system,' he went on.

Pat blew her nose.

'Why, love? Why have you changed your mind now?
Just tell me. We'll do whatever you want to. We won't
go if you really hate the idea. Just tell me.'

Pat looked at him through her red eyes. His face was
indeed very round and innocent. She wondered that she
had never noticed that before. He was simply another
disappointed young bank clerk. Another man in a
dead-end job, with an average wife, a few drinks on a
Saturday, two nice, but time-consuming and money-
swallowing children, a car that needed a lot of money
spent on it, or else needed to be replaced. They had a
loan of a caravan each year, but he would never feel the
sands of the West Indies or the Seychelles between his
toes.

She began to speak and then stopped. She must be
very careful now. It was as if he had been a negative,
and now somebody had shown her the developed print.
She could see all the frustrations, the hours of commut-
ing, the thickening of his waist. Those things were far

18

from the James Bond or Wild West books he read for a half-hour before he went to sleep each night.

A surge of understanding went out from her. He just needed some excitement, something out of the ordinary, some proof that he wasn't a mouse, that he was going to do something daring in his life before he grew old and retired and walked with a stick and crumpled and died.

Quite calmly she looked at him and said:

'I'm jealous. That's it. That's the truth.'

'You're what?' he said.

'I don't want them, to have you, to see you. I don't want those girls to . . . you know, make free with you. I'd be very jealous. I love you. I don't want them loving you.'

'But Pat,' he said desperately. 'We've been through all this; it's got nothing to do with love. It's got to do with swapping. It's got to do with excitement, and frontiers . . . and not doing the same thing always . . . till the end of our days.'

She had been right. She resolved that she would do everything her feeble imagination and some sex manuals could dream up if only they got home unscathed from Seven Sisters.

'You're too great,' she said hesitantly. They didn't use flowery endearments, they never paid each other extravagant compliments. It was hard to begin on a street in the middle of the evening in North London on the way to a wife-swapping orgy. But people have to begin somewhere.

'You're too . . . important. Too precious, and exciting. I love it when we . . . er . . . screw. I don't want other women to share it. It's my . . . er, pleasure.'

'Do you love it?' he asked innocently.

'Oh I do,' she closed her eyes, a sigh of genuine pleasure that she might in fact be going to win escaped her, and it sounded like genuine desire.

'I didn't think you minded all that much one way or another,' he said.

19

'If you knew how I do,' she said. And then firmly, 'But I wouldn't feel at all the same if you let all these women crawl over you . . .'

She paused. It was a calculated risk. In fact she had given little thought to Stuart's part in the whole sorry business, she had been obsessed with her own role. But she thought that to say this would have been to confirm Stuart in thinking that he had married parochial, puritan riff-raff and that his excitement would be between the covers of books for the rest of his days.

'I often . . . er . . . get panicky in case some of the women who come into the bank might . . . er, proposition you,' she said.

Stuart looked at her.

'There's no need to worry like that. That's kind of paranoid that jealousy,' he said soothingly. 'I've always been faithful to you. Even this business tonight is *with* you.'

'I don't want to share you with them,' she said. 'I'm not going to. They've got lousy old husbands, awful fellows. I've got you. Why should I be so generous?'

He paused. He looked up the road, he looked down the road. Her eyes never left his face. Down the road won.

'Suppose we got a couple of kebabs . . .'

'And a bottle of wine.'

As they turned to go back to the station, a middle-aged couple stopped in a car to ask them where the Road was.

Pat asked them what number they wanted.

As she had suspected, it was number 17.

'Have fun,' she said as she gave them directions, and she and Stuart dissolved in laughter.

'They were a bit old,' said Stuart. 'Do you think it would have been very sordid and sort of pathetic?'

Pat wasn't going to let him think that.

'No. There were probably fabulous birds there. Anyway, older ones are more passionate. She'd probably have had you pinned to the hearth rug the moment we got in the door.'

Under a street lamp, she thought his face looked a bit foolish. As if he had seen how tatty and grubby it might all have been. He was very gentle. In a great wave of affection she realized that indeed she would not have liked sharing him with anyone, and that an evening in bed with a bottle of wine, and a nice spicy donar kebab and all that black and red underwear might be the most exciting kind of thing that she had experienced for some time as well.

Women are so much more sensible about sex, she thought cheerfully as Stuart bought the tickets home. She had forgotten the weeks of anxiety, the endless examinations in the mirror, the ceaseless fears lest anyone should discover. Heady with relief she even allowed herself the indulgence of imagining what that elderly woman in the car might look like naked, and she smiled at Stuart who looked like a tiger now that his wife was too rabidly jealous to allow him indulge in the wife-swapping party to which they had been invited. Horizons had been broadened without anyone having to do anything.

Finsbury Park

Vera hated to see television plays about poverty. She even disliked seeing working-class women, babies in their arms, hair in rollers, explaining some social problem to a concerned television reporter. It reminded her too much of her youth. In those shuffling, whiney women she could see her mother, cigarette always hanging from the corner of her mouth, cardigan held together with a safety pin, the door of the flat never closed since people were always coming in and out, the place smelling of clothes drying . . . clothes that had not been properly washed so it was really dirty clothes drying.

Vera hated to hear women laugh loudly, they reminded her of her mother and her elder sister, cackling away when things were at their worst, cheering each other up with bottles of ginger wine and announcing that they would be dead long enough. Vera never liked to think of anything that reminded her about life as it was lived before she was fifteen.

On her fifteenth birthday she was taken to the hospital with rheumatic fever, and during the long weeks there she got to know Miss Andrews, the gentle school teacher in the next bed who changed her life.

'Ask them to bring you lavender water not sweets.'
'Ask your school friends for hand cream not comics.'
'I'll choose some nice books for you from the library.'
'We'll tell the social worker you'd like a hairdo to cheer you up . . . .'

The Vera who came out of hospital was slimmer and

attractive looking. And she had changed inside too. Miss Andrews had taught her a very important lesson – even awful things and unhappy times can have their uses, they can be a kind of apprenticeship. Vera must stay at school, she must pass some kind of exams even if school was hell and home was worse than hell.

She had closed her eyes to the dirt and depression around her. She had dreamed of the day she would live in a clean house with no frying pans encrusted with the remains of a thousand meals. She dreamed of having a room to herself where no noise and no shouting could be heard, where no younger sister with nits in her hair would bounce on her bed saying:

'It's half my room, you can't throw me out.'

'Don't leave too soon,' Miss Andrews had begged. 'Don't go until you are sure you can support yourself. It would be too depressing to have to return there. That would break your spirit.'

Vera found it difficult to remember the two years she stayed on in her mother's flat. She knew that her father must have come home from time to time . . . the period seemed to be punctuated with screaming and violence. She must have learned something at the school because she had managed to escape with some 'O' levels. And during those two years she must have formed the habit of visiting Miss Andrews once a week, some hundred calls must have been made to the quiet apartment with its piano, its dried flowers, its cabinets of china and its purring Persian cat.

As an apprenticeship it must have worked, but it was blotted out. By the time Vera had finished, she could type, she could take shorthand, she could spell. Miss Andrews had taught her to smile and to speak nicely. Not in actual lessons, but by example. Vera's voice was less shrill, her vowels less extreme, her reactions less speedy – so much so that her mother was totally unprepared for her flight from the tenement. It was done without fuss, without argument and without heed to the pleas.

'You'll come back often to see us, you'll come home every weekend,' begged her mother.

'Of course,' said Vera, and never did.

She sent her mother an envelope with a card and a pound in it three times a year, Christmas, birthday, and mother's day. No details of how she was or where she was. No plans about coming back for a visit. No enquiries about the rest of the family. They had no way of telling her, when Margaret died. And no way of appealing to her when Colin was lifted by the police. And when the pound had reduced to a fifth of its value she still sent it. Crisp and green, attached by a paper clip to a non-commital card of good wishes. Once her mother tore it up and threw it into the fire. But Vera was never to know that.

Miss Andrews had been too genteel, too ladylike to reveal to Vera what she later discovered to be a major truth in life – that money was the solution to almost every problem. If Miss Andrews had known this she hadn't thought of passing it on, and after Vera had cut her ties with the family she also stopped seeing Miss Andrews. To the teacher she sent more thoughtful cards, and sometimes a lace handkerchief or a little sachet for her drawer. She never said what she was doing or where she was, and soon, or at some time anyway, the lonely teacher put Vera out of her mind. There was a finality about her three-line notes . . . they said goodbye.

Throughout her first five years of freedom, which also meant five jobs and five different bed-sitters, Vera still regarded herself as in apprenticeship. There was no time for dalliances like every other girl she worked with seemed to have. There was no money to waste on silly things – the cinema, yes, sometimes, if it was the kind of film that might teach her something, about style, clothes, manners. Mainly British films, American style was too foreign, it might be outrageous, it might not even *be* style. Lunch hours spent in fashion stores, or in bookshops, reading but not buying the magazines;

money, after the rent was paid, spent on evening classes in everything from Beginner's French to Grooming.

Suddenly she was twenty-three, and nicely spoken and well informed and living in an attractive bed-sitter. She had collected some pretty ornaments, not unlike those that Miss Andrews had in her glass-fronted cabinet. She knew extremely important things about not mixing styles in her decor. She had learned as if by rote some rules of elegant living and if she had ever given herself the opportunity to entertain anyone she was absolutely confident about how the table should be set and what wines to serve with each course.

She had never relaxed about her background, and was amazed that other girls, the kind she met at work, would talk so freely about the uncouth habits of their parents . . . and joke about the vulgarity of their backgrounds. Vera would never be drawn. Once or twice when people did press she said that it hurt her to talk about the past. And people assumed that there had been some tragedy or some unpleasantness and left it at that.

Because of her interest in china she got a job running the gift shop of a smart hotel and it was here that she met Joseph. Twenty years her senior, with his big anxious eyes and his worried face, he was the ideal catch, one of the giggling receptionists had told her. A lonely widower, no children, pots of money, so broken up after his wife's death that he had sold the house and moved into a hotel. He had been living in this hotel for three years. He was apparently looking for a wife, since hotel life had its drawbacks. Sometimes he called at her little shop to buy gifts for clients, always she advised him with charm and taste. He was very attracted to her. Soon he managed to find the courage to ask her out. Vera's own hesitation was genuine. In her effort to become her own version of a lady, she had given very little time to recognizing that she was a woman. She knew little of men, and was very shy on their first few outings. This pleased Joseph more than anything else she could have done . . . In a matter of weeks he was telling her of his dream house, but his fears of being lonely in it if he bought it for himself alone. She agreed with him enthusiastically, she thought that a big place was bad if you were alone. That's why she only had a tiny bed-sitter.

Joseph wondered if he could come and call at her bed-sitter some time. Vera agreed and asked him for afternoon tea the following Saturday. The sunlight caught the beautiful china, and the gentle highlights in Vera's hair, and the shining wood of the one small table . . . and Joseph's eyes filled with tears. He started to apologize for being forty-five, and to excuse himself for his arrogance in supposing that a beautiful young girl could possibly . . . She let him babble on for some minutes and then just as he was about to retract everything he had said from sheer embarrassment, she laid a finger on his lips and said,

'Don't say any more, Joseph. I should love to see your dream house in Finsbury Park, and we'll make it the most wonderful palace in the world.'

She had heard dialogue a little like that in some old movie, and it seemed right for the occasion. It was indeed. Utterly right. The months passed in a flurry of inspecting the house, giving in her notice at the hotel, accepting a small marriage settlement from Joseph, a complete refusal on her part to have anything to do with her family, a quiet wedding, an undemanding honeymoon in the sunshine of the South of France and then Vera's apprenticeship ended and her life began.

The small scullery attached to the great kitchen in Finsbury Park became her headquarters. Here she sat and studied the plans, here she returned after great measuring trips around the rooms, here she studied fabrics, paint charts, samples of tiles, wood pieces. It was in this scullery that the catalogues began to mount up as she debated, and wondered and frowned, and pouted, and looked at the first ones again. Joseph began to fret after a few weeks.

'Is it proving too much for you, my little darling?' he asked anxiously. 'You know we can have a designer, and a consultant if you like. Someone who will take the donkey work from you.'

'Donkey work?' cried Vera in genuine amazement. 'But this is the best bit. This is what we want, to decide it ourselves, to have it perfect. To have a perfect house which we get for ourselves!' Her eyes looked almost wild with enthusiasm, so Joseph decided not to point out that they slept on a bed in a bedroom, and ate meals in the little scullery while a fourteen-room house awaited them. It was like a naked house waiting to be dressed.

It got dressed. Amazingly slowly. It took months for the painting, months for the curtains, the furniture to build up. Two years went by and it still looked as if they had just moved in. Joseph was deeply disappointed.

He worked hard all day as a company lawyer. He had thought that his life had taken a new and almost miraculous turn when the flower-like Vera had agreed to marry him. True, his evenings were less lonely than when he lived in the hotel. But they were a lot less comfortable. In the hotel he had room to rest, to relax, room to work. In the hotel he had excellent food. At home, in the future palace, he had no room. He lived from a box in their bedroom, since Vera would allow no furniture anywhere until it had been finally agreed and settled and each item took months. The cooking was negligible since they had to wait for all the equipment to be installed. Vera didn't seem interested in food, she didn't seem to think he needed it either. She rushed to greet him on his return each day with a peck on the cheek and a sheaf of leaflets and swathes of fabric.

'Oh there you are, my dear. Dearest, so you think this flower is too large. I'm not quite certain, I'm almost certain but not quite.'

He began to try and guess what she wanted him to say, but knew that he had to give the pretence of ruminating over it, otherwise she would not be satisfied.

27

Often, faint with tiredness and hunger after two hours of studying design, he wondered whether she might in fact be having some kind of nervous trouble that he hadn't noticed before. Then he would banish the thought guiltily, and tell himself that he was a selfish swine to expect his young wife to have a glass of scotch ready, a meal cooking and a lively interest in his day.

Sometimes he called at the hotel and ate before he came home. Vera never seemed to mind. Yes, of course she had plenty to eat, she made herself cups of soup and sandwiches she said vaguely.

Joseph's hope that they would have children was also doomed. It was a long time before he realized that Vera had been taking the contraceptive pill. All this time he had been hoping that she would tell him she had conceived.

'But darling we can't *think* of children in this beautiful house. I mean how could you have children with this wallpaper?' Her hands caressed the wallpaper almost sensuously.

'But not ever?' gasped Joseph shocked.

'Perhaps sometime,' Vera said distantly aware she might have gone a little too far.

Vera was twenty-eight, they had been five years married when he dared to say to her that the house was perfect. He had admired every single item, rearranged every piece of furniture with her and now he hoped that the endless business was over. To his increasing alarm he noted that she didn't seem too anxious to spoil the kitchen by cooking, and she didn't want to fade the colours in the sitting room by letting the light in. There was no comfortable fug in the study she had designed for him, because she begged him not to have the heating too high lest it blister the paint. His cigar smoking was done outside his own home.

That was the unhappiest year of Joseph's life, because he now realized that the completion of the house did not signal the start of a normal life together. Her attractive face was still bent over magazines and fabric charts. They had never entertained anyone. He had taken his mother, an elderly woman there once . . . for a drink before Sunday lunch. Vera said she couldn't possibly cook a huge Sunday roast if they were to show the kitchen at its best.

'But why do we have to show it, at its best?' he begged.

'Why spend all this time and money unless we want things at their best?' she answered.

He hoped that if he got her some regular help she might become more relaxed about it. Together they interviewed seventeen applicants, the wages he offered were high. Eventually she settled on a Filippino girl with as much interest in the house as she had herself. Together they cleaned and polished all day. Together Vera and the little Filippino washed woodwork, and held the fitments of glass lights in soft dusters rubbing gently till they shone. The little girl from Manilla saved every penny she earned, and drank packet soups with Vera all day to keep up her strength. At night she went to her own room, and watched a portable television. Vera had bought her this in order to keep her at home. She told Joseph that if Anna went out at night she would lose her energy for polishing.

Joseph suggested a cook as well, but Vera asked why did they want someone to mess the place up. She would however like a daily woman to do the heavy work so that Anna and she could be free to do the finer chores.

The cleaning woman came five days a week. She thought Vera was daft and told her so. Vera didn't even listen. She certainly didn't feel insulted.

'If you don't like the job and the money, I'll get someone else,' she said reasonably, without any offence in her voice.

The cleaning woman was called Mrs Murray, and she lived in a block of flats not at all unlike the ones where Vera had grown up. Sometimes Mrs Murray feeling a bit sorry for this poor madwoman she worked for, would tell tales of Life in the Buildings. Vera's face contorted with near spasms. She almost ran from the room if Mrs Murray began to evoke the life and sounds.

'Please, Mrs Murray, I beg you, go on with your work. I don't want to delay you. Another time.'

Behind her back Anna and Mrs Murray pointed to their own foreheads and shook their heads.

'I think she must have had nothing when she was young,' said Mrs Murray one day in a burst of confidence to Anna.

'I always think she very wealthy lady,' said Anna.

'Wouldn't you feel sorry for her old man?' Mrs Murray went on. 'He'd be better off down with us, coming in to a bit of a laugh and a good meat pie, and a block of ice cream with a glass of port after it, and his slippers. I think that's what he'd prefer, to tell you the God's honest truth.'

Anna gave it some thought.

'Yes, and when I think of my family back in Manilla . . . where there is little money . . . and little food and little furniture . . . but when the father comes in . . . all stops and there is smiling and welcoming and he is an important man.'

Mrs Murray nodded sagely.

Outside the door, where she had paused, not to eavesdrop but to polish the corner of a picture frame which had escaped them all, Vera stood and listened. Her body was flooded with a great pity for them. Two poor women, not much older than herself. One from a drunken Irish family, living now in slum conditions in a London council flat, one a poor Asiatic whose family and country were so wretched they had to export her to clean floors and send them back her wages.

And these two women pitied her. Vera gave a high-pitched little laugh at the wonderful way that nature allows people to bear their burdens so easily by considering themselves better off than others. Happily she moved from the door and knelt down to examine the ball and claw feet of the table which were known for their ability to trap dust.

Highbury & Islington

'I hope you'll like them all,' he said for the fourth time.

'Oh, I'm sure I will,' said Heather without looking up.

'I think you'll get on with them,' he said, anxiously biting his lip.

Heather raised her eyes from the magazine.

'I said I'm sure I will, funny face. Even if I don't it's not the end of the world. They don't have to live with me, I don't have to live with them.' Cheerfully she leaned over and kissed him on the nose. Then she took off her shoes, settled her feet in his lap and applied herself seriously to her magazine. A very colourful looking one with a lot of Sin and Passion and Frenzy in capital letters on the cover.

Adam hoped that she might have finished the magazine and, better still, have thrown it away before they got home. He could see his mother's amazement – Frenzy and Sin magazines weren't forbidden at home, it was just that nobody would contemplate buying them. He could imagine his sister's sarcastic comments. Louise was always a little sardonic about strangers but he felt unhappily that Heather might give plenty of ammunition.

'*A trifle bookish I see, your Heather?*' Louise would shout as she retrieved the offending magazine. And, oh God, would Heather relax so thoroughly that she would actually sit in her stockinged feet as she was doing now?

Adam looked out of the train window, and fixed his

31

face in what he hoped was a calm, pleasant expression while he tried to work out some of the more glaring problems which faced him at the weekend. He had explained to Heather that there could be no question of sharing a bed under his mother's roof. She had accepted it good-naturedly.

'No point in terrorizing the poor old darling is there? I'll wait until they've all had their Ovaltine then I'll slip along to wherever you are.'

He had even managed to tell her that this would not do either. He painted a picture of a home with three women, Mother, Louise and old Elsie; this was the first time any guest had been invited to stay; there would be enormous excitement. There would be amazing scrutiny. Heather had sounded disbelieving but shrugged.

'Well, two nights' denial won't kill us.'

Adam had read a lot about love before he had met Heather. He knew only too well that love was often unreturned – as in the case of his loving Jane Fonda for a while. She had simply been unaware of his existence. And nearer home there had been a severe case of unreturned love when he had yearned for that stuck-up girl in the dramatic society. Of course, he too had been loved, by that mousey friend of Louise's; the quiet little girl with the irritating cough and nervous laugh. She had loved Adam for a bit and was always pretending that she had been given two theatre tickets and asking him would he like to come to plays with her. He hadn't loved her even a little bit.

Heather was his first experience of Real Love, and Adam frowned as he looked into people's houses from the train window. Real love often ran into problems, well, from Romeo and Juliet onwards. There were cases of families refusing to countenance young lovers. He didn't think this would happen at home. Mother and Louise wouldn't summon old Elsie from the kitchen and face him with an ultimatum. It would be very different and much harder to take . . . they would laugh at Heather, and ridicule his taste. In little ways they would call attention to her shortcomings; they would assume that she was a tasteless little dalliance on his part. They couldn't know that he loved her and wanted her more than he had ever wanted anything in his life.

He moved her feet slightly, she looked up and smiled at him over her torrid magazine.

'Dreaming?' she asked him affectionately.

'A bit,' he said and felt a wave of disloyalty flooding him. Love wasn't meant to be like this, it had nothing to do with trying to get two sets of people to make allowances, to change, to bend in order to accommodate each other. Love was meant to be straightforward. If things got in the way of love, then the Lover had to remove them, honestly and with integrity and dignity. The Lover wasn't meant to sit gnawing his fingers about the confrontation of those that he loved.

He had known Heather for a year and he had loved her for eight months, but this was the first time he had ever raised enough courage to take her home for a weekend. It hadn't been easy.

'But of course you can have a friend to stay, darling,' Mother had said. 'Who is he? Anyone we know?' Mother had an idea that she might know anyone of substance in London. Among the twelve million people Adam could meet, she felt sure that the one chosen to be a friend might be someone she knew.

'A girl. How dramatic!' screamed Louise pretending to be a Victorian Lady overcome with shock. Adam could have wrung her neck with pleasure. 'Is she a débutante? Do tell, do tell.'

Adam had explained that Heather had a bed-sitting-room in the same house in Islington. He did not go into the fact that for the past few months they actually shared the same bed-sitting-room so as to save rent. To the eager faces of Mother and Louise, and of Elsie who had come in from the kitchen at the noise of all the excitement, he announced that she really *was* just a friend, and that he would love to invite her for a weekend. He begged them not to ask people around for sherry on Sunday morning. He implored Elsie not to give the place a thorough spring clean before young Mr Adam's young lady came; he said that honestly Louise shouldn't save her supper party for the tennis club people until Heather arrived. Short of going on bended knees he couldn't have done more to ask for a quiet, normal weekend. It had, of course, been useless.

It was only natural that they should be so interested in his doings, Adam thought forgiving them, loving them for caring so much. Since Father died he was the only man in their life; Louise was too bookish, too brisk for men. Well, she was nineteen and had never shown any real interest in men. She worked in the local library, she never mentioned boyfriends. She couldn't have any secretly, could she? After all she lived at home. Every second weekend Adam arrived home to the Sussex town, and told them tales about his life in London. The work in the bank, his prospects. His squash games, his walks on the Heath. The little pub theatres he went to, his French classes preparing for big banking opportunities in the E.E.C.

He mentioned lots of friends by name, but never Heather. He said nothing about the discos they went to on the Saturdays he stayed in London. He thought Mother might find discos a bit, well, lower class, and Louise would ask in her penetrating voice: 'But why, Adam, why do people go to rooms with loud music and funny lights which eventually ruin their eyesight – I mean, do they enjoy it, Adam?' He told Elsie that he was learning a little bit more about cooking, but he didn't explain that it was Heather who taught him, Heather who said: 'I made the supper last night, you'll bloody do it tonight mate or I'll find myself a bloke who believes in equality.'

34

His worlds were so different that he had put off for as long as he could the date when they had to be brought together. Adam who sat down with a linen table napkin to tasteless, overcooked, plain food served from cracked china plates behind heavy net curtains . . . and Adam who sat on the bed with a great wooden bowl of highly spiced chili, a bottle of red wine on the floor, his arm around Heather as they laughed and watched television. In the summer evenings the window of their basement flat was often open for all to see . . . He could hardly believe they were the same person.

Heather had invited him to her home several times. Her stepfather had asked Adam for a loan of a pound on each occasion and Heather had cheerfully shouted at him not to be so daft. On one occasion Adam had secretly slipped the man a pound, hoping to buy his affection, but in fact it only worsened relations between them as Heather had said it would. Heather's mother was a hard-working Scot. She looked Adam up and down and said she hoped that he was a man who could hold down a day's work. Adam explained nervously that although he was still a lowly bank official he was indeed a regular worker and had great ambitions. Heather's mother said she approved of that because she herself had been unlucky in that she had married two wasters and two scroungers and two men who would drink the Thames Estuary dry if they got a chance. 'There were only two altogether, Mam,' Heather had said laughing. 'She always makes it sound as if there were six!'

Adam couldn't understand the casual bond that held the mother to her daughter. It wasn't love, it had nothing to do with duty. There was no need involved, it didn't seem to matter whether Heather went home for months or not. There were no recriminations, no inter-rogations. There didn't even seem to be a great deal of interest. Heather's mother could hardly remember the name of the department store where Heather worked.

Adam marvelled at that; Mother and Louise and Elsie knew the name of every under-manager and a great many of the customers in his bank.

Heather had always seemed amused about his tales of home. But then, Adam wondered with mounting horror as the train was taking them ever nearer, had he told accurate tales? Had he let her know just how very formal Mother could be? Heather hadn't thought of taking a gift for the weekend, so Adam had bought a potted plant.

'You can give that to Mother,' he had said.

'Why? I don't know her. She'd think it was silly,' said Heather.

'No, first time meeting her, she'd think it was nice,' he insisted. 'It's what people do, honestly.'

'You didn't take a plant to my Mum,' she said reasonably.

Adam was furious. He hadn't taken a plant to Heather's mother because she lived forty minutes away on the tube, because they had gone there for tea one Saturday, because Heather had said that her mother hated airs and graces and he hadn't wanted to be considered a young dandy. Now it was being used against him.

He thought about the kind of weekend they could have had if they had stayed in London. The cinema tonight, perhaps, and a fish and chip supper. Saturday morning poking around antique shops and second-hand stalls. Drink a few pints with some of Heather's friends at lunchtime . . . the afternoon would pass in a haze of doing up the room they lived in, sweeping the leaves away from the basement gutters; they might carry on with that picture framing; they might go and drink a bottle of wine with other friends until they went to the disco; and instead he had this torture ahead.

The train stopped and his heart lurched; they couldn't be there yet. Surely there was another half-hour.

'Are we there?' Heather yawned and rooted for her shoes. She hadn't a hint of nervousness or anxiety. She reached for his carefully chosen potted plant.

'Don't forget your geranium,' she said.

They hadn't arrived, but they had reached a situation which called for their having to change trains. That was how the guard put it.

'Has this one broken down?' Heather asked him.

'It is a situation where you have to change trains, Madam,' he said again.

'I'd love it if he was in charge of any crisis,' grumbled Heather getting out on to the platform. Her eyes lit on the Ladies Room. 'I'll take advantage of the change of train situation to have a relief of bladder situation,' she said happily and scampered off to the lavatory.

Adam stood glumly wondering why he thought everything that Heather said was funny and endearing at home in London and he thought it was coarse and offensive when he was starting to get into Mother's orbit. He leaned against a telephone box waiting for Heather to come back from the Ladies and for the next train to come and rescue them. On the opposite platform stood lucky people going to London. They would be there in time to go to a theatre perhaps, they might be salesmen coming home from some conference in Brighton. None of them had forty-eight hours of anxiety lying ahead of them as he did. None of them had to worry about Mother asking Heather, 'And what school were you at my dear?' and Louise asking Heather, 'You mean you actually sell things to the public? Heavens!', Elsie asking Heather, 'Would you like Earl Grey or English breakfast in the morning?' He winced and felt a real pain at the thought of it. And there was no way he could muzzle Heather and ask her to remain completely silent, so she was bound to talk about times when they had both been pissed and to let slip that they had smoked pot, and lived in the same room, and that her father had

37

died in an alcoholics' home and her step-father was bankrupt . . .

Adam heaved a very deep sigh.

Love was turning out to be full of problems that the poets and the movie makers never spoke of.

Suddenly he thought he couldn't stand it. Not now, not yet. He wasn't ready to take the weekend now. Perhaps later when he and Heather were so sure of each other and of their happiness that a weekend like this wouldn't matter. Perhaps later when he didn't seem like a small boy wet behind the ears to the Mummy and the Sister and the Old Retainer . . . perhaps then Adam's Bohemian lifestyle and friends would be much more acceptable. Perhaps when he was more of a man.

He knew he had to act in the next minute if he was going to stop the disastrous visit. A quick phone call . . . he was most most dreadfully sorry but he had just come down with this dreadful flu, and Heather had sent her regrets and would so look forward to meeting Mother and Louise and everyone another time. Yes, yes he could do it now quickly. And to Heather? Well imagine how funny life is! He had just phoned home to explain that they were going to be late and, fancy, Mother had come down with this dreadful flu and had been trying to contact him, could they possibly put off the visit? Then he and Heather had only to cross the platform, jump on a London bound train. In an hour or two they would get off at their tube station, and, hand in hand, clutching their weekend bags and the geranium, they would go home . . . there would be no hurts, no confrontations. Love would remain separate and self-contained. He could be a loving son every second weekend until he was mature and manly enough not to care.

With one hand on his ear to cut out the noise of the trains he told the tale first to Elsie and, gritting his teeth trying to put out of his mind her tones of disappointment, he agreed to tell it all again to Mother.

'We had everything so nice,' Elsie said, 'We even had

a fire in Miss Heather's bedroom. Your mother had the chimney swept during the week.'

Mother was concerned about his imaginary flu, but he had the strangest feeling she didn't entirely believe him. She gave the merest of hints that she thought something more exciting and glittering had turned up for Adam and Heather.

'Don't go out to any parties or occasions now, if you have flu.'

There was something about the way his mother used the work 'occasions' that brought a prickle of tears to Adam's eyes. It was as moving as Elsie being disappointed not to see Miss Heather's pleasure at the fire in her bedroom. Mother thought that bank clerks and shopgirls were good worthy people in service industries . . . but she thought of her son Adam as being 'in banking' and she assumed that his nice friend Heather was a young lady who would indeed be invited to glittering functions.

'I'm sorry, Mother,' he said.

'Adam my dear, you can't help having influenza,' said Mother, and he could hear Louise in the background saying: 'Oh no, you don't mean after all this they're not coming. It's too bad.'

Fiercely he told himself that it was better this small hurt than two days of misunderstanding and misery. Then Heather came swinging easily along the platform.

'Any news on the train?' she asked.

He told her about his sudden call, his mother's flu, her deep regrets, he added that there had been a fire in her bedroom. Heather looked at him levelly.

'Yes, really, a fire in your bedroom, Mother had got the sweep to come in and do the chimney specially during the week,' he said, desperate that she should understand how much welcome had been prepared. After Elsie and Mother's pain he couldn't bear it if Heather were flippant.

'I see,' she said at last.

'So, we can just go back, back to London, we can cross the footbridge there,' he said reading the sign aloud.

'Yeah, that's right,' said Heather.

'And we're really only losing the cost of the ticket,' he said eagerly looking at her. 'That's all we're losing.'

'Sure Adam,' she said, but he knew from her voice that he was losing a great deal more. He had known that from Mother's voice too. For once in his life, Adam wondered if there were a danger that he might *never* grow up.

King's Cross

Eve looked around the office with a practical eye. There was a shabby and rather hastily put together steel shelving system for books and brochures. There were boxes of paper still on the floor. There was a dead plant on the window, and another plant with a Good Luck in Your New Job label dying slowly beside it. The venetian blind was black – there was so much clutter on the window ledge it looked like a major undertaking to try and free the blind. One of the telephones was actually hidden under a pile of literature on the desk. In the corner was a small, cheap and rather nasty-looking table . . . which would be Eve's if she were to take the job.

And that's what she was doing now, as she sat in the unappealing room . . . deciding if she would take the job of secretary to Sara Gray. Sara had rushed off to find somebody who knew about holidays and luncheon vouchers and overtime. She had never had a secretary before and had never thought of enquiring about these details before she interviewed Eve. She had pushed the hair out of her eyes and gone galloping off to personnel, which would undoubtedly think her very foolish. Eve sat calmly in the room waiting and deliberating, by the time Sara had bounded back with the information, Eve had already decided to take on Sara Gray. She looked like being the most challenging so far.

Sara heaved a great sigh of relief when she heard that Eve would stay and work with her. She had big kind brown eyes, the kind of eyes you often see shown close up in a movie or a television play to illustrate that someone is a trusting, vulnerable character and therefore likely to be hurt. She looked vague and bewildered, and snowed-under. She sounded as if she needed a personal manager rather than a secretary – and this is where Sara Gray had hit very lucky because that's what Eve was.

From the outset she was extraordinarily respectful to Sara. She never referred to her as anything but Miss Gray, she called her Miss Gray to her face despite a dozen expostulations from Sara.

'This is a friendly office,' Sara cried. 'I can't stand you not calling me by my name. It makes me look so snooty. We're all friends here.'

Eve had replied firmly that it was not a friendly office. It was a very cut-throat company indeed. Eve had asked Sara how many of the women secretaries called their male bosses by their first names. Sara couldn't work it out. Eve could. None of them. Sara agreed reluctantly that this might be so. Eve pressed home her point. Even the managers and assistant managers on Sara's level were not going to escape, they all called Sara by her first name because she was a woman, but she felt the need to call many of them Mr. After two days Sara decided that Eve must be heavily into Women's Lib.

'There's no need to fight any battles on my behalf, Eve,' she said cheerfully. 'Look at how far I've got, and I'm a woman. Nobody held me back just because I'm a downtrodden put-upon female. Did they? I've done very well here, and I get recognition for all I do.'

'Oh no, Miss Gray, you are quite wrong,' said Eve. 'You do not get recognition. You are the assistant promotions manager. Everyone knows that you are far better and brighter and work much harder than Mr Edwards. You should be the promotions manager not the assistant.'

Sara looked upset. 'I thought I could say I'd done rather well,' she said.

'Only what you deserve, Miss Gray,' said Eve who seemed to have acquired a thorough familiarity with the huge travel agency and its tour operations in two days. 'You should have Mr Edwards' job. We all know that. You *must* have it. It's only fair.'

Sara looked at her, embarrassed.

'Gosh Eve, it's awfully nice of you, and don't think I don't appreciate it. You're amazingly loyal. But you really don't know the score here.'

'With great respect, Miss Gray, I think it's you who doesn't know the score,' said Eve calmly. 'It is absolutely possible for you to have Mr Edwards' job this time next year, I'll be very glad to help you towards that if you like. I have a little experience in this sort of thing.'

Sara stared at her, not knowing what to say.

'Miss Gray, I'm going for my lunch now, but can I suggest you do something while I'm gone? Can you telephone one or two of the people on the list of references I gave you? You will notice they are all women; I've never worked for men. Ask any one of them whether she thinks it's a good idea to trust me to help. Then perhaps you might add that you will keep all this very much in confidence . . .'

'Eve,' interrupted Sara, her good-natured face looking puzzled, 'Eve, honestly, this sounds like the mafia or something. I'm not into power struggles, and office back-stabbing . . . I'm just delighted to have someone as bright and helpful as you in the office . . . I don't want to start a war.'

'Who said anything about a war, Miss Gray? It's very subtle, and very gradual and – honestly the best thing is to telephone anyone on that list, it's there in the file marked Personal.'

'But won't they think it rather odd. I mean, I can't ring up and ask them what do they think of Eve trying

43

to knock Mr Edwards sideways so that I can get his job.' Sara sounded very distressed.

'Miss Gray, I have worked in five jobs, for five women, I chose them, they thought they chose me. At the very beginning I told them how a good assistant could help them get where they wanted. Not one of them believed me, I managed in a conversation like this to convince them to let me.'

'And . . . what happened?' asked Sara.

'Ask them, Miss Gray,' replied Eve, gathering her gloves and bag.

'They won't think I'm er . . .'

'No, all of them – except the first one, of course – rang someone else to check things out too.' Eve was gone.

Sara wondered.

You often heard of women becoming a bit strange, perhaps Eve was a bit odd. Far too young to be menopausal or anything, heavens Eve wasn't even thirty, but it did seem an odd sort of thing to suggest after two days.

Was there a wild possibility that she might have had a secret vendetta for years against Garry Edwards, the plausible head of promotions, who indeed did not deserve his job, his title, his salary or his influence, since all of these had been made possible only by Sara's devoted work?

Sara reached for the phone.

'Sure I know Eve,' said the pleasant American women in the big banking group. 'You are so lucky, Sara, to have her. I offered her any money to stay but she wouldn't hear of it. She said her job was done. She acts a bit like Superman or the Lone Ranger, she comes in and solves a problem and then sort of zooms off. A really incredible woman.'

'Can I . . . er . . . ask you what problem she . . . er . . .' Sara felt very embarrassed.

'Sure. I wanted to be loans manager, they didn't take

me seriously. Eve showed me how they would, and they did, and now I'm loans manager.'

'Heavens,' said Sara. 'It's a teeny bit like that here.'

'Well naturally it is, otherwise Eve wouldn't have picked you,' said the loans manager of a distant bank.

'And how did she . . . um . . . do it?' persisted Sara.

'Now this is where I become a little vague,' the pleasant voice said. 'It's simply impossible to explain. In my case there was a whole lot of stuff about my not getting to meet the right people in the bank. Eve noticed that, she got me to play golf.'

'*Golf?*' screamed Sara.

'I know, I know, I guess I shouldn't even have told you that much . . . listen, the point is that Eve can see with uncanny vision where women hold themselves back, and work within the system without playing the system properly so – she kinda points out where the system could work for us, and honestly honey, it worked for me, and it sure as hell worked for the woman who Eve worked on before me, she's practically running industry in this country nowadays. In her case it had something to do with having dinner parties at home.'

'What?' said Sara.

'I know, it sounded crazy to me too, and I got real uneasy, but apparently she needed to show people that she could sort of impress foreign contacts by having them to a meal with grace and style and all pizzazz in her country home. Eve sort of set it up for her with outside caterers and it worked a dream. You see, it's different for everyone.'

Sara was puzzled. She walked down to the local snack bar and bought a salami sandwich. She ate it thoughtfully on the road coming back to the building. In the lift she heard that Garry Edwards was going to a conference in the Seychelles next week. It was a conference for people who brought out travel brochures, a significant part of promotions for any travel firm. Sara had done all the imaginative travel brochures, Garry

Edwards had okayed them. Yet he was going to the Seychelles and she was eating a tired salami sandwich. When she opened her office door Eve was sitting there typing.

'I'll do it,' she said. 'Whatever it is, play golf, give foolish dinner parties . . . I'll do it. I want his job. It's utterly unjust that he's going to that conference, it's the most unjust thing I've ever known.'

'He won't be going to it next year,' said Eve. 'Right, Miss Gray, I have a few points ready to discuss with you, shall we put this sign on the door?'

'What is it?' Sara asked fearfully.

'It merely says, "Engaged in Conference," I made it last night.' Eve produced a neat card which she then fixed on the outside of the office door.

'Why are we doing that?' whispered Sara.

'Because it is absolutely intolerable the way that people think they can come barging in here, taking advantage of your good nature and picking your brains, interrupting us and disturbing you from whatever you are doing. We need a couple of hours to plan the office design, and it's no harm to let them see immediately that you are going to regard your job as important. It may only be half the job they should have given you, but don't worry, you'll have the right job very soon.'

'Suppose that the really big brass come along, or Mr Edwards or you know, someone important.' Sara was still unsure.

'We are having a conference, about the redesign of your office.'

'But there isn't any money to redesign it . . . even if they'd let me.'

'Yes there is, I've been up to the requisition department, in fact they looked you up on the book, and wondered why you hadn't applied. Whenever you're ready Miss Gray, we can start.'

Together they worked out how the office should look. It was a big room, but it was in no way impressive; apart from the inferior furniture, its design was all wrong: Eve explained, that a separate cubicle should be built for her near the door. Eve should act as a kind of reception area for Sara, she should call through to announce visitors, even though it was only a distance of a few yards.

'They'll walk past and come straight on in,' said Sara.

'Not if I walk after them and ask can I help them. They won't do it twice, Miss Gray,' said Eve and Sara realized that most of them wouldn't even do it once.

The costing of the partition was not enormous, and it left a reasonable amount for the rest of the furnishings.

'We'll have the filing section in my part since you shouldn't really have to be looking things up yourself, Miss Gray, but it will of course be kept in a very meticulous way so you can always find anything.'

'What will I have in my part of the office then?' asked Sara humbly.

Eve stood up and walked around. 'I've been giving it a lot of thought, Miss Gray. You are really the ideas woman here. I'm sorry, I know it's jargon, but that's what you do for the promotions department. You thought up that whole idea about choosing a holiday from your stars in the zodiac and that worked, you thought of having a travel agents' conference in that railway station which suited them all since they had to come from all over the country and go back again by train. You thought up the scheme of having children write the section for children's holidays, so I think that this is what you should be doing really. Thinking. And let me handle the routine things, you know, the letters about "Can you trace what we did about Portugal two years ago?" If the filing system works properly then anyone will be able to do that for you. I'll set it up so that at least four-fifths of your incoming mail can be handled by any competent secretary. That should give you a great deal more time to do what you are really good at.'

Sara looked hopeful but not convinced.

47

'Me just sit in here with a chair?' She shook her head. 'I don't think it's on Eve, I really don't. You know they'd think I'd gone mad.'

'I wasn't suggesting a chair. I was going to suggest a long narrow conference table. Something in nice wood, we could look at auctions or in an antique shop. And about six chairs. Then, for you a small writing desk. Again something from an old house possibly, with your telephone and your own big diary and notebook, a few periodicals and trade magazines or directories you need, that's all.'

'Eve, in God's name, what is the long conference table for. Eve, I am the assistant promotions manager, not the chairman of the board. I don't give conferences, call meetings, ask my superiors to come in here with the hope of blinding them about policy.'

'You should,' said Eve simply. 'Listen,' she went on. 'Remember that children writing the brochure idea? It was marvellous. I've been looking through the files, you got not one word of credit, no letter, no mention, no thanks even. I would not be at all surprised if you, Mr Edwards and I are the only people who know you thought it up, and the only reason I know is that I see entries in your diary about going to schools and talking to children and spending a lot of your free time working on it. Edwards got the praise, the thanks and the job, for not only that but for everything you did. Because you didn't do it right.'

'It worked, though,' said Sara defensively.

'Miss Gray, of course the idea worked, it was brilliant, I remember seeing those brochures long before I ever knew you, and I thought they were inspired. What I mean is that it didn't work for you, here within the company. Next time, I suggest you invite Mr Edwards and his boss and the marketing director and one or two others to drop in quite casually – don't dream of saying you are calling a meeting, just suggest that they might all like to come into your office one afternoon. And then, at a nice table where there is plenty of room and plenty of style, put forward your plans. That way they'll remember you.'

'Yes, I know, in theory you're right, Eve ... but honestly, I'm not the type. I'm jolly old Sara Gray, with a nice, jolly, hopeless lover who comes and goes at home – and who is gone at the moment. And they all say to themselves, "poor Sara, not a bad old thing" – none of them would take me at a rosewood conference table for one minute Eve, they'd either corpse themselves laughing or else they'd think I was having a breakdown, they'd fire me. And you.'

Eve didn't look at all put out. 'I wasn't suggesting calling a conference tomorrow, I was suggesting having the furniture right. If you are someone who is valuable to the company for her ideas, you should have a space to think up these ideas, a platform to present them on, and the just recognition for them.'

'You're right,' Sara said suddenly. 'What else?'

'I think you should get into the habit of having Mr Edwards and others coming to this office, by appointment of course, rather than you rushing to theirs. It makes you more important. That's why we need the right furniture. Mr Edwards has an office like an aeroplane hangar, and very well laid out, I've inspected it. But yours could have a charm, it could become the place where ideas were discussed say on one particular evening a week, a Thursday, before people left. It would be relaxing, and pleasant, and *you* would be in control.'

As they talked on, it got darker outside, and they switched on the bright neon overhead light.

'That'll have to go for a start,' said Eve. 'It's far too harsh, there's no style, no warmth.'

A few times the door had been half-opened, but whenever people saw the two heads bent over the desk and lists, they muttered apologies and backed out.

'I never thought a notice would do that,' said Sara admiringly.

49

'Wait till we get things going properly, you'll be amazed.' said Eve.

Eve refused a drink, a girly chat and the offer of a share in a taxi. Instead she took out her notebook again.

'You should have an account with a taxi firm,' she said briskly. 'I'll set that up tomorrow, when I'm organizing the flowers and your dress allowance.'

Sara stared at her in the windy, wet street as if Eve had gone completely mad.

'*What* are you organizing . . .?' she began.

'Plants, flowers for the office, all the male senior executives have them, and they also get a special expense allowance for clothes because they have to travel, it being a travel company, and . . . .'

'Eve, I'm not a senior executive, I can't have free flowers paid for by the office.'

'As assistant manager you are technically a senior executive. The other two assistant managers are elderly men who have been pushed upstairs, so if you equate your title with theirs then you can have flowers, nothing extravagant, about six nice flowering plants. I think we can choose them from a brochure, they'll arrive tomorrow.'

For the first time for a long time Sara sat back contentedly in her chair at home and didn't think about Geoff and wonder when his new obsession would end. Often she felt lonely and sad during his absences, so that she would hide from the feeling by having the television on or listening to music for long hours. But tonight she just sat calmly drinking her tea and looking into the fire. Eve's arrival meant that a lot of the tension in the office had been eased. It was like someone massaging your shoulders and taking away the stiffness – you didn't know how tense you had been until the massage was over – Eve was going to make things a lot better, and she was going to force Sara to take herself more seriously too. It was a bit exciting in a way.

Next morning was a Friday and Eve wanted to know whether Sara had any important plans and engagements for the weekend. Sara shrugged 'I was going to sort out those figures for Mr Edwards, you know the ones he wanted on the breakdown of age groups on the coach holidays. We need to know where to direct some of the coach tour promotions this year.'

'Oh, that's done.' said Eve. 'I did it this morning, I saw his note. I've two copies here for you to sign, one for Mr Edwards and I thought you should send one to the head of marketing, just to let him know that you are alive and well and working harder than Mr Edwards.'

'Isn't that a bit sneaky?' asked Sara looking like a doubtful schoolgirl.

'No, it's standard office procedure. Mr Edwards is the sneaky party, by not acknowledging your part in all the work that is being done.'

With a weekend free Sara agreed happily to go to look at second-hand furniture and office fittings. Eve had already organized the office partition, and it began with great hammering and activity after lunch.

'I suggest you go and check out a few new outfits for yourself, Miss Gray,' said Eve. 'You can't possibly work here with all this noise.'

'Could you come with me, I'm not exactly sure what I . . .?'

'Certainly, Miss Gray, can you wait five minutes while I tell these gentlemen I shall be back in two hours to see how they are getting on?'

Eve managed to make three large men look as if they knew she was going to have them fired unless the partition was perfect. Then she went to the shop with Sara.

There was a brief objective discussion about what clothes Sara already possessed. Eve explained that she had only seen two tweed skirts and one black sweater in the three days she had been working there. Shamefacedly, Sara said she thought there were a couple of other sweaters and perhaps two more workable tweed skirts.

Eve seemed neither pleased nor put out; she was merely asking for information. In the store she suggested three outfits which could interchange and swap and make about a dozen between them. They cost so much that Sara had to sit down on the fitting-room chair.

'I took the liberty of getting you a credit card for your expenses, Miss Gray,' said Eve. 'I rushed it through, and what you are going to spend now is totally justifiable. You have to meet the public, you have to represent the company in places where the company may well be judged by the personal appearance of its representatives. What you are spending on these garments is half what Mr Edwards has spent in the last six months, and you have been entitled to expenses of this kind for over a year and never called on them.'

By Monday Sara could hardly recognize either herself or her new surroundings. On Eve's advice she had had an expensive hair-do; she wore the pink and grey wool outfit, put the pink cyclamens on her window sill, near the lovely old table with its matching half-dozen chairs which they had eventually found for half nothing since it was too big for most homes, and nobody except Eve would have thought of it as office furniture.

Eve was living in her purpose-built annexe surrounded with files and ledgers. She had just begun to compile a folio of Sara's work so far with the company, a kind of illustrated *curriculum vitae* which would show her worth and catalogue her achievements. Nobody was more surprised than Sara by all she seemed to have done during her years in the company.

'I'm really quite good, you know,' she said happily.

'Miss Gray, you are very good indeed, otherwise I wouldn't work with you,' said Eve solemnly, and Sara could detect no hint of humour or self-mockery in the tone.

Towards the end of the second week, Eve pronounced herself pleased with the office. She had bought an old coat-stand which ideally matched the table and chairs, and on this she urged Sara to hang her smart coat so that the whole place just looked as if it were an extension of her own creative personality. If anyone gasped with amazement at the changes in the room, Sara was to say that there was all this silly money up in requisitions for her to decorate the place, and she did hate modern ugly cubes of furniture so she had just chosen things she liked – which had in fact been cheaper. People were stunned, and jealous, and wondered why they hadn't thought of this too.

Remarks about her appearance Eve suggested should be parried slightly. No need to tell people that she now had regular twice weekly sessions with a beautician. Eve had booked her a course of twenty.

So on the second Friday of her employment Eve came into Sara's part of the office and said she thought that they were ready to begin.

'Begin?' cried Sara. 'I thought we'd finished.'

Eve gave one of her rare smiles. 'I meant begin your work, Miss Gray. I've been taking up a lot of your time with what I am sure you must have considered inessentials. Now I feel that you should concentrate totally on your work for promotions and let me look after everything else. I shall keep detailed records of all the routine work that I am doing. Each evening I'll leave you a progress report, too, of how I think we have been getting on in our various projects. These I think you should take home with you or else return to my personal file. We don't want them seen by anyone else.'

Sara nodded her thanks. Suddenly she felt overwhelmed with gratitude for this strange girl who was behaving not as a new secretary but as if she were an old family retainer blind with loyalty to the young Missie, or a kindergarten teacher filled with affection and hope for a young charge.

She felt almost unable to express any of this gratitude because Eve didn't seem to need it or even to like it.

'Are there any, er, major projects you see straight away?' she asked.

'I think you should look for an assistant, or a deputy, Miss Gray,' said Eve.

'*Eve*, you can't go, you can't leave me now!' cried Sara.

'Miss Gray, I am your secretary, not your assistant. I certainly shall not leave you for a year. I told you that. No, you need to train someone in to do your job when you are not here.'

'Not here?' Sara looked around her new office which she was beginning to love. 'Where will I be, why won't I be here?'

'Because you will be away on conferences, you will be travelling abroad to see the places the company is promoting, and of course, Miss Gray, you will be taking your own vacation, something you neglected to do last year I see.'

'Yes, but that'll only be a few weeks at most. Why do I need to have an assistant, a deputy? I mean it's like empire building.'

'You'll need to train an assistant to take over when you get Mr Edwards' job at the end of the year. One of the many reasons why women fail to get promotion is because management can say that there is nobody else to do their job on the present level of the ladder. I suggest you find a bright and very young, extremely young man.'

'But I can't do that. They'd know I was plotting to get Garry Edwards' job.'

Eve smiled. 'I'm glad you are calling Mr Edwards by his first name at last, Miss Gray. No, you need an assistant to do your work for you while you are away, of course. Otherwise, if this whole office is seen to tick along nicely without you in your absence, people will wonder why your presence is so essential. If on the other hand, it turns into total chaos, they will blame you *in absentia*. So you need a harmless, enthusiastic, personable young man to sign letters which I will write and to postpone anything major until your return.'

'Eve, why do you have to go away in a year?' Sara said suddenly. 'Why can't you stay and together we'll take over the whole place. Honestly it's not impossible.'

'Oh, Miss Gray, there'd be no point in taking the place over. It's not what either of us want, is it?' asked Eve, accepting naturally that it would be perfectly feasible to takeover the largest travel company in Britain if she put her mind to it.

'You never tell me what you want,' Sara said, impressed by her own daring.

'I like to see women getting their work recognized. There's so much sheer injustice in the business world – I mean really unjust things are done to women. I find that very strange. Men who can be so kind to stray dogs, lost strangers, their own children, contribute generously to charities and yet continue appalling unfairness towards women at work.'

She stopped suddenly.

Sara said, 'Go on.'

'Nothing more,' Eve said firmly. 'You asked me what I wanted. I want to see that injustice recognized for what it is, and to see people fight it.'

'You should write about it, or make speeches,' said Sara. 'I never even saw it in my own case until you came. I do agree now that I've been shabbily treated and now I've got a bit of confidence to demand more. And that's only after ten days with you. Think what success you'd have if you were to go on a lecture tour or on television or something.'

Eve looked sad.

'No. That's just the whole trouble. It doesn't work that way, damn it. That's why it's going to take so long.'

Politely she extricated herself from further explanations, from any more conversation, from having a drink at a near-by pub with Sara. She had to go home now.

'You never tell me about your home,' said Sara.

'You never tell me about yours, Miss Gray, either,' said Eve.

'I would if I got a chance,' Sara said.

'Ah yes, but you and I would not get on so well if I knew about your worries and problems!'

Sara took it as a very faint warning. It meant that Eve didn't want to hear about Sara's problems and worries either. She sighed. It would have been very helpful if Eve could apply her amazing skills to Sara's disastrous relationship with Geoff. He had been gone now three weeks. No, it couldn't be three weeks. It was. She could hardly believe it. The last ten days has passed so quickly she had scarcely missed him. She was so stunned by this that she hadn't heard what Eve had said.

'I was only saying that I left your invitation for the supper party tomorrow night there on your desk,' Eve repeated as she gathered up her things. 'I hope you enjoy it. I heard that all senior executives were normally invited to meet the chairman and board members so I made sure your name was on the list. Nice chance to wear that black dress too, Miss Gray, I expect you're thinking.'

Sara's eyes were big with gratitude. As if by magic Eve seemed to have known that another lonely weekend was looming ahead. But she knew not to admit to any emotion.

'Great. I'll go in there and knock them dead. And on Monday we'll be ready to begin the campaign.'

'Excellent,' said Eve. 'I suggest you find out whether any of the board have young and hopefully stupid sons who might want to start in the business. As your assistant, you know. We need someone rather overeducated with no brains.'

'What are you going to do for the weekend?' asked Sara.

'This and that, Miss Gray. See you Monday,' said Eve.

Sara spent Saturday reading the company's reports which Eve had left thoughtfully on her desk. She took Eve's advice and wore the black dress to the party where Garry Edwards' surprise at seeing her was as exciting as any romantic flutter. 'I can see how people can become obsessed with all this infighting and competitiveness,' thought Sara.

She was charming to the chairman, she was respectful to Garry Edwards and risked calling him Garry once or twice: she caught him looking at her sideways several times. She was very pleasant to a middle-aged and lonely woman who was the wife of a noisy extrovert board member. The woman was so grateful that she positively unburdened her life story. Eve's face came like a quick flash across the conversation; Sara remembered how she had implied that people don't really want to be bogged down with personal life stories, particularly of a gloomy nature. She murmured her sympathy for the details and disclaimers of the woman's tale about neglect and being pushed into the background.

'All he cares about now is our son, he's coming down from Cambridge soon, with an Arts Degree: no plans, no interests.'

Eve would have been proud of her. She geared the conversation gently to her own office, to how she would be delighted to meet the boy – she even gave the woman her card with a little note scribbled on it. How amazing that she should suddenly find a need for those nice new cards which Eve had ordered for her and produced within days of her arrival. Garry Edwards came across at one stage to find out what she was up to; Sara steered the conversation away again.

'Where's that chap that you are seen with sometimes – and sometimes not?' asked Edwards, determined to wound.

'If he's not here, it must be one of the evenings I'm not seen with him,' said Sara cheerfully.

That night she went to sleep in her big double bed, hoping that Geoff would not come home. She had too much to think about.

The weeks went by, two more of them. She had already held three successful and supposedly impromptu gatherings in her office. Always she had included several people higher in the pecking order than Garry Edwards.

Everyone had thought it was a splendid idea to have the handsome young son of their important board member and his lonely wife in the department. He worked most of the time in the general promotions department and two afternoons a week he got what was described as a training from Sara. What it really was was an access to her files, permission to sit in her room as she worked out schemes with some of the other promotions executives, and he learned an almost over-powering respect for Miss Gray from Eve who stood up and expected him to do the same. Eve almost lowered her voice in awe when she spoke of anything Sara had done, and the well meaning, over-educated and not very bright Simon did the same.

Simply because Eve kept him under such an iron rule Simon did learn something. So much in fact that his parents were utterly delighted with him, and the head of marketing, who had opposed his appointment as the nepotism it undoubtedly was, had to admit that that young Miss Gray was able to do the most extraordinary things. He took to dropping in to her pleasant office occasionally, and once or twice that strange colourless secretary had told him very firmly that she couldn't be disturbed. When he implied that he was more impor-tant than whoever she could be talking to, the secretary had said very flatly that her instructions were to ask everyone to make appointments, or at least to tele-phone in advance if they intended to drop in. Since the head of marketing had been saying long and loud that too much socializing and twittering went on in his

department in the name of work he could not be otherwise than pleased.

Geoff came back. His latest lady decided that she
must go back to her husband and children. This she said
was where her duty lay. She said it when all Geoff's
money had run out. Geoff had shrugged and come back
to Sara. Amazingly she wasn't at home. He let himself
in one night with a bottle of champagne, a single rose
and a long explanation, but there was nobody to receive
any of these things so he just went to bed.

She wasn't there in the morning either. He checked
her wardrobe, most of her sweaters and skirts seemed
to be there. The place looked neater somehow, and
there were no work files strewn about. She had a lot of
much more expensive cosmetics in the bathroom too.
He wondered what had been happening. He couldn't
have been gone more than a month. She hadn't run out,
surely? She couldn't have decided to end with him,
surely? After all she hadn't changed the lock or anything. His key still opened her hall door.

He called her next morning, and a very cool voice
that was not Sara's answered him. 'Miss Gray's office.'

'Oh we have gone up in the world,' giggled Geoff.
Loyalty to Sara and building her up to her colleagues
was never his strong suit.

'I beg your pardon?' said the voice.

'Listen, it's Geoff here, can I talk to Sara?'

'Can I know who wants to speak to Miss Gray
please?' asked Eve.

'Hell, I've just told you. It's Geoff. Sara's chap,
Geoff. Put me onto her will you, sweetheart.'

Eve answered very pleasantly. 'I'm afraid you must
have the wrong number.'

Geoff sounded annoyed, 'Sara Gray's office, right?'

'Yes this is Miss Sara Gray's office, now will you
kindly tell me who this is speaking?'

'Geoff. Geoff White, for Christ's sake, who is that?'

'I am Miss Gray's secretary. Mr White can you please

tell me your business. You're taking up a lot of time.'

She didn't actually lie when Sara asked had Geoff phoned. She said that a totally inarticulate man had called but it could hardly have been Geoff. Sara had only paused momentarily to wonder. She had spent five days at a sales conference in Paris, and had told Eve excitedly how she had been asked to address the meeting twice about new brochure ideas. Mr Edwards – or that buffoon Garry as she was now calling him – looked positively yellow with rage. He had tried to make a pass at her which she had rejected with amazement and something akin to distaste. Eve was full of praise.

Next day Sara said: 'The inarticulate man must have been Geoff. His things were in the flat, but I couldn't bear to be woken at three a.m. with champagne and tears and all, so I bolted my door and didn't hear whether he called or not.'

Eve nodded in her cool way. She wanted to hear no more, not one word of Sara's private life. Yet she looked pleased. Things were going as hoped for. Sara was now too busy to worry about Geoff, and soon she would be too confident to accept his amazing behaviour which was already a legend in office gossip. The new Sara would either throw him out or make him behave in a civilized way. Very satisfactory.

The weeks passed again. By now it was already office gossip that Sara would shortly take over from Garry Edwards. People who hadn't rated her much before, were saying now that she had been holding back. Others said that she was always brilliant and that it was only a matter of time before it was recognized.

Garry Edwards blew it. He tried to drop Sara into great trouble for one of his own mistakes. Unlucky Garry Edwards that he had joined battle with Eve's filing system, the relevant documents were produced in a matter of minutes; quite obviously Sara had dealt with the problem, had recommended a correct course of action.

It was shortly after this that Eve asked Sara to come into her small cubicle and go over the filing system with her.

'Let's do a test,' Eve said. 'Suppose you had to find Press Comment on Senior Citizen Campaign, where would you look?' Sara checked first under 'publicity' then under 'Senior Citizens'. It took her five minutes.

'It's too long,' said Eve firmly. 'Perhaps you should have a look for something every day for the next month or so. Just to familiarize yourself.'

'You're going to leave me aren't you?' asked Sara.

'I think so,' said Eve.

'It's not the year, it's not even half a year,' Sara complained.

'But there's nothing left to do, Miss Gray. We get you a new efficient typist, we both explain to her and to Simon what the routine is, you'll be leaving shortly anyway for Mr Edwards' job, we'll just make sure that any changeover here goes smoothly.'

'Can't you come with me, upstairs?' Sara nodded in the direction of the promotions manager's office. 'Please.'

'No, you can do it better on your own really. And it's better for you.' She was like a swimming instructor encouraging a bright but apprehensive pupil.

'The office, Eve, how will I do up the office so that its like this . . . I mean I hate his furniture, I hate his style.'

'You choose, Miss Gray. A few months ago you wouldn't even have noticed his office or his style.'

'Eve, a few months ago you know very well nobody would have noticed me.'

'You underestimate yourself, Miss Gray. Shall I advertise for a secretary, I'd be happy to advise you on any points during any interview.'

'God, yes Eve,' Sara looked at her. 'I won't keep asking you but you know there's no problem about salary.'

Eve shook her head.

Sara put her face into a bright smile. 'In a few months

61

I suppose I'll get a telephone call from some bewildered woman asking me do I know Eve and can I possibly recommend her insane notions.'

Eve looked solemn. 'Well, yes, if you don't mind. I should like your name as a reference.'

'And I'll say Miss whoever you are ... Eve is not from this planet. Let her have her way with you and you'll be running your company in months.'

Eve stood up briskly. 'Yes, if you think it was all worth it.'

Sara put out her hand and held Eve's arm.

'I know you hate people prying but why, just why? You're far brighter than I am, than the woman in the bank, than the other woman – the one you told to have dinner parties. I mean, why don't *you* do it. Why don't you do it for *you*. You know better than any of us how to get on. It's like a kind of crusade for you but you stay in the background all the time. I don't know what you're at. What you want.'

Eve shrugged politely. 'I like to see you do well, Miss Gray, that's enough reward for me. You deserve it. You were being passed over. That wasn't just.'

Sara nodded. 'Now I promise, all the rest of the time you are here, I'll never ask again. Never. Just tell me. Why this way? If you feel there's discrimination against women there must be better ways to fight it.'

Eve leaned against the beautiful table and stroked it. 'If there are I can't find them. I simply know of no better way to fight it than from within. You have to use the system. I hate it but it's true.'

Sara didn't interrupt. She knew that if Eve was ever going to say anything it would be now. She let the pause last.

'How do you think I, as a feminist, like asking intelligent, sensitive women like you and like Bonnie Bernstein in the bank, and Marrion Smith in the ministry to dress properly? As if it mattered one goddamn whether you wore woad to the office ... all three of you are worth more than any man I ever met in any kind of business. And I could say that for seven or eight other women, too. But women don't have a chance, they don't bloody know . . .'

Sara sat breathless.

'It's so *unjust*.' Eve stressed that word heavily. 'So totally unjust. A married man has a woman to look after his appearance and his clothes and his meals and his house, a woman does not. A single man has a fleet of secretaries, assistants, manicurists, lovers to look after him. A single woman is meant to cope. A man is admired for sleeping with people on his way up, a woman is considered a tramp if she does. A man . . .' She paused and pulled herself together, almost physically. 'Miss Gray, you must excuse me. I really don't think I should be taking up your time with all this. I do apologize. I feel ashamed of myself.'

The moment was gone, the spell was broken.

'I don't suppose you'll tell me why you feel like this? I mean was there some experience in your life, Eve, you are so young, too young to be bitter about things.'

Eve looked at her. 'No, of course I'm not bitter, I'm very constructive. I just try to get some justice for strong, good women who deserve it. When I've got it I move on. It's very satisfying. Slow but satisfying. Now, about this advertisement. I don't think we should phrase it "travel business", it will attract the kind of woman who thinks in terms of cheap flights and free holidays.'

Sara played along. She owed Eve that much.

'Oh yes, of course. Let's word it now, and put it in whenever you want to. The later the better of course. You know I don't want you to leave here ever.'

'Thank you very much, Miss Gray. But I think really if you agree I'll get it into tomorrow's papers.'

Sara looked up.

'So soon?'

'There's a lot to be done,' said Eve.

Euston

Elizabeth marvelled at the changes in Euston. She remembered the station much more clearly as the fairly gloomy and barracks-like place where she had gone with Mother and Father to meet Dara each year when she came over from Ireland on holiday. And here she was years later in the huge revamped place with its shops and its flashing lights and escalators waiting for Dara again. Dara who could well afford to fly but who decided that it would be more fun to retrace the old tracks and come on boat and train; Dara who had always made the holidays turn into technicolour for Elizabeth, the only child; Dara who was so quiet and gentle but somehow managed to make things cheerful in a house where there was little love; Dara who had been able to say things to Mother and Father even after one of their dreadful rows – something that would ease the atmosphere – while Elizabeth would sit mute and tight-lipped, afraid that by opening her mouth she would drive her parents further from each other than they already were.

Even after the divorce, when she and Dara were fifteen, there had been a visit. Mother and Elizabeth had waited in this very spot and when Dara got off the train and ran up to them, she had hugged Mother and said; 'You poor old thing, it must be desperately lonely and sort of low for you these days,' and Mother had hugged her back and cried. Mother crying in public and hugging Dara.

Elizabeth had felt her heart lift for the first time since the divorce. Dara always had this gift of saying what people didn't say and it all worked perfectly.

During that particular visit Dara had suggested that she would like to see Father. Dara said she had a present for him from Ireland. Mother had pursed her lips and looked disapproving. Elizabeth had feared that everything was going to turn sour again. 'Aw, come on out of that,' Dara had said. 'Now for the rest of your life you can't be expecting that nobody except Elizabeth is going to want to be friends with both of you. It's not a battle for us.'

And because of Dara the visit to Father had been marvellous instead of stilted, and Dara had said 'Aw, come on out of that, of course you've got a new lady friend, why can't we meet her? It's silly to ask her to be out all day, or hidden away as if she were in disgrace.' So Father, delighted, had suggested that Julia join them for lunch, and it had been a memorable meal with wine and a sip of brandy afterwards, and Dara said that there was no purpose in carrying tales from one household back to another, it only made things worse on everyone . . . and with her carefree attitude she had brought some kind of happiness into that troubled summer also.

Dara lived in Ireland with an old grandmother, a housekeeper and a gardener. Her parents, who had been friends of Mother and Father in the old days, had been killed in a car crash and so now Dara's life was a matter of cycling to a local school each day, coming home and making sure her hands were nice and clean and that she came in to lunch or dinner when the gong sounded. She told her old grandmother little tales about what happened at school or with her friends, or during the holidays about what she had read. She seemed to lead an idyllic existence, wandering around the countryside exploring and reading in her large sunny bedroom which looked out on purple mountains. Once a year she came to spend two weeks in London, her annual treat.

The friendship lasted long after schooldays. Dara had trained as a nurse in an Irish hospital at the same time as Elizabeth was doing her training in London. They still holidayed in each others' homes, and as they became more adventurous they even went as far as Spain and Italy together. When Dara's grandmother died there was even talk of her coming to London to share a flat with Elizabeth but she said she would miss the purple mountains and the narrow roads, which she now drove along in her little car instead of pedalling on her creaking bike.

There was also a question of Dara marrying some doctor near-by. Elizabeth had become very excited about this and hoped the romance was going well.

'Do you think he's interested? Do you really think he's contemplating it?' she had asked Dara eagerly when she went to spend a spring week in the Irish countryside and had met the handsome doctor two or three times.

Dara had astonished her by saying: 'Oh, that's not the point. I mean it's easy enough to make him interested, it's just that I don't know yet if *I* want him or not. That's the only problem.'

Elizabeth had been mystified. She assumed in some vague way that Dara must be talking about sexual favours, but despite their years of friendship this was not an area that they discussed. The young doctor was dropped from conversation and from Dara's life, and always Elizabeth had a suspicion that Dara may have loved him a lot, but had failed to attract him. That her conversation had merely been bravado. Still, Dara seemed to have few regrets. She had transformed her grandmother's crumbling old house into an excellent old people's home. The housekeeper and the gardener lived there in style and comfort to work out their old age in payment for all they had given to the place. This

66

gave Dara a very high reputation in the community. Many a young one who came into money might have been hoity-toity, but Miss Dara was different. A very kind young woman indeed. She employed a small staff, all of whom seemed to have been chosen on grounds of their pleasant personalities. It wasn't surprising that the place had a waiting list of several years. Dara kept a supervisory eye on the place but she still worked some hours in the local hospital and still took time to travel. People often wondered why she didn't marry. By the time she was thirty-five they assumed that she was a career woman. It couldn't be from lack of suitors or opportunities.

Elizabeth, too, wondered from time to time, why Dara had never married. But it had not been a serious worry. She assumed it was because of the gentle fulfilling pace that Dara's life always seemed to have been lived at. She had never been searching or seeking. She was always perfectly content with her lot. That's what had made her such a delightful companion. Perhaps these Irish men who must surely have fancied her had been too diffident, too unsure in their own minds about the whole concept of marriage to force Dara to change, to insist that barriers be broken down. Dara would have made a great wife and sailed through all the storms of matrimony, Elizabeth sighed as she waited at the station.

And there were many. Oh dear Lord, there were many. It was a simple fact that when you get married there are not enough hours in the day. Nothing more or less. There are not sufficient slots of time to be a wife, full of interest and concern, and dying to make love, and up to date with every aspect of Derek's work in research. To be a mother, wiping dirty faces, washing clothes, playing creative games, spotting incipient infections, participating meaningfully in the playgroup scheme, arranging baby-sitters that will get on well with the children. To be a worker, to put in thirty-eight hours a week in the nursing agency. To be a home maker, that awful American word which seemed to cover a full-time job polishing, shining, making curtains, cooking, entertaining, gardening. Even if she slept only two hours a night, Elizabeth thought, it would be too much. There were not enough *hours*.

She needed the job, they both needed her to have the job. Derek's job was not well enough paid for the kind of lifestyle they wanted. Anyway, she liked the job. What she didn't like was the constant guilt, the foolish wearying feeling of being behind at everything. She hated taking the children's mending to work to try and do it in the crowded bus, but where else could she find that spare half-hour? She hated shopping at lunch hour, she hated having to rush and pick the children up from a neighbour's house and have them at home demanding her time and attention before she had time to unpack the groceries and have a shower. It would only take her half an hour, that extra half-hour would give her so much more freedom and energy, but it was impossible. Her bus passed the neighbour's house at five-thirty so it made sense to pick the children up there and walk the ten minutes home with them rather than coming back and having an extra twenty minutes added to the evening at the other end of a half-hour's peace at home. Or so Derek had said. Derek came home at seven, when the house was invariably a mess, the children and herself locked in some struggle about bed, toys, bath, supper. It had become so wildly unsatisfactory that Elizabeth was feeling severe strain, and because of her small medical knowledge she knew it was teetering near the edge of a breakdown.

She wrote it all out in a long letter to Dara, wondering whether she should just collapse and let it all take care of itself. Dara said she would come for a month. Elizabeth could spend a week in a nursing home, two weeks in a health farm and one week at home picking up the threads.

'I'll come at the beginning of February,' Dara had written. 'By March 1st you will be right as rain.'

It was as if a Messiah had announced an imminent coming. Elizabeth was happy already.

When Dara came bouncing up the ramp, her short brown hair ruffled and attractive, Elizabeth felt an almost physical pain of relief. Here was the one person who would make the household happy again. The great restorer of peace as she had been in Mother and Father's time, doing it over twenty years later for Elizabeth herself. She hugged her and clung to her with tears starting to flow.

Dara was obviously startled to see her friend in such poor shape. She put her hand professionally on Elizabeth's forehead.

'I see I'm just in time,' she said. She waved them into a taxi airily. 'You're in no shape to battle with the tube, silly,' she said. 'Anyway we can make our plan of campaign in comfort. Have you booked the nursing home?'

'Yes,' gulped Elizabeth. 'I think they must think I am not all there. It's very dear.'

'That's my wedding present to you, I never gave you a proper one,' said Dara. Elizabeth had a vague memory that Dara had given her some huge fluffy towels but she said nothing.

'Now, the health farm the next week.'

'Yes, yes. I booked it. I know you said to take it from Mother's legacy, I have. Do you think two weeks is too long?'

'No,' said Dara. 'Now Derek. Have you told him yet?'

'Well, yes and no,' said Elizabeth, her face becoming twisted in an effort to explain.

'That means no,' said Dara.

'He'd think I was silly, he'd think I was weak and self-indulgent.' Elizabeth began to stutter in her eagerness to defend Derek's attitude. 'You see, I've been so hopeless recently. So tired. And so complaining. I don't want to let him think he married a dud.'

'Tell him your doctor insisted on it,' said Dara. 'I'll back it up, and say in my professional opinion, which is true by the way, I never saw anyone so much on the verge of collapse. I'll run the house, mind the kids, give Derek his bowl of porridge now and then, and when you come back glowing and well you'll be as right as rain.'

That lovely expression, 'as right as rain', Elizabeth had used it a million times, without ever thinking about it. She thought suddenly of the soft gentle rain in Ireland. She thought about the constancy of rain. She felt vastly cheered.

'I don't know why you came to meet me,' said Dara. 'I could easily have made my own way to the house, you know. It would have given you another couple of hours to yourself.'

'Oh we always meet you at Euston,' said Elizabeth, and Dara patted her hand affectionately.

The house was indeed in poor shape. Dara looked around with a practised eye. The children were sweet little three- and four-year-olds, Benny and Nell, but they had obviously worn Derek to a frazzle.

'What *do* they eat at this time darling?' he said in a harrassed tone to Elizabeth. 'They seem very restless. I've no idea what you should have given them.'

Dara gave Derek a peck, and vanished to her room. She returned in ten minutes dressed for work in a simple pinafore of green corduroy.

'You look very business-like,' said Derek with approval. Elizabeth felt even more foolish in her best silk suit, which she was hoping might escape the strains and dangers of Benny and Nell.

'Well your wife is going to leave us together for three weeks, I'll tell you all about it later,' she said. 'So meanwhile, I suppose I'd better dress to please you.'

Already the tension was lifting.

Already the atmosphere was lighter.

Dara was working her familiar magic.

70

'Lie down, Elizabeth my love, I'll call you when the meal is ready. Do, there's a good girl,' said Dara.

And Elizabeth went up to her room, where she rested with a great sense of relief. Dara would explain it all to Derek. Dara would make him see that she wasn't a non-starter. Not a weakling. She closed her eyes. At peace for the first time for ages. It was nine o'clock when Dara came to waken her with a cup of consommé with sherry.

'This will liven you up,' she said.

Elizabeth drank it gratefully.

'What's happening? I must get up,' she said suddenly.

All her guilt came flooding back. The meat hadn't been unfrozen for the goulash, the dish-washing machine hadn't been emptied. Heavens. There might well be no clean linen. She had been asleep for two hours.

'It's under control,' said Dara. And indeed it was. Derek had been banished with a drink to the television, the children had been bathed and given cornflakes, the goulash had been designated tomorrow's dinner, while Dara's smoked salmon from Ireland had been carved and sliced and laid on beds of vegetables, the table had been polished and old mats with hunting prints had appeared. In the kitchen the soft whir of the washing machine meant that all the table linen as well as the children's clothes were purring around in a low suds detergent. Elizabeth sighed with pleasure. It was a delightful dinner, and Derek said to her tenderly that he felt very selfish for not having noticed her strain. All three of them made great plans for the week in the nursing home. They drank a toast to the joy of hospitalization without any disease, or any terror of waiting for results. For the first time in months Elizabeth slept a long peaceful sleep.

Elizabeth went to the nursing home early in the morning. Derek drove her there before he went to work. Dara said she knew well the running of the house, and insisted that she could also replace Elizabeth at the nursing agency so that no extra cash would be lost. The real reason she wanted to do it was to ensure that nobody there could regard Elizabeth as a malingerer. Dara's nursing qualifications were even superior to Elizabeth's, there would be no problem.

And indeed there *were* no problems.

Dara realized quickly that a great deal of problems could be solved by buying food in bulk. So she made a master list and suggested that she and Derek buy this early on Saturday morning. She settled him with the children in a café and had the shopping ready to be collected from the supermarket door in forty minutes. Then she settled in to sit with the children while she sent Derek with a list to buy the week's drink and gardening requisites. 'That's a man's job,' she said when Derek demurred, and he felt very important.

On Sunday she arranged to have the neighbour's children for the day, mainly so that they would entertain Benny and Nell in the bedroom which she had made into a play room for them. But it also made the neighbour feel that she wasn't being taken for granted. It meant she could go to the pub and even have a leisurely lunch with her husband and a bit of slap and tickle. She agreed readily to hold on to Benny and Nell until whatever hour the family liked to collect them on work days. 'I think Derek should pick them up in his car. Their little legs get tired walking home,' said Dara. Derek wondered why nobody had ever thought of this.

She spent a half-hour each day in the garden, but always in places where it showed. The front looked weeded and cared for. Dara even organized funny winter window boxes which looked cheerier than anything else on the road.

When Derek arrived home with the children, she was there, cheerful, fire lighting, and drink in her hand. Derek relaxed while she bathed the toddlers, and together they read them funny stories while they had

72

their supper and went to bed. Then Derek and Dara played chess or looked at television while she mended clothes. Dara told Derek funny tales of the people she nursed. She always made the people sound tender or witty or eccentric, never demanding or tiresome. He loved to hear of them. She was very interested to know where his research was going and why so much money was being given to the Americans while so little went to the British.

Each night they telephoned Elizabeth and listened to what she said. Sometimes she seemed very defensive, and self-justifying. 'You don't have to explain to us,' said Dara over and over. 'We know why you're run down. It's a killer running a job and a home.' Yet, Dara didn't look killed by it, she glowed with happiness, and the house seemed to turn on oiled hinges.

The day of Elizabeth's return was to be fêted, Dara decided. There would be a special celebration meal. Elizabeth was to come back at seven o'clock on a Friday.

'Be sure to take a taxi from the station, darling,' said Derek. He was beginning to believe that a small expense on taxis could save a lot of wear and tear and a lot of time.

Benny and Nell made a banner with 'Welcome Home Mummy' on it. There was to be a bottle of champagne and a cake. They all sat until nearly eight o'clock when Derek became worried and rang the health farm.

'Oh, she left here this afternoon,' the director said. 'She should be with you by now.'

The key turned in the lock and in from the wet sleet came Elizabeth dripping on the newly vacuumed floor.

'I took the tube, a taxi seemed such a waste. Then there were no buses,' she said.

There were cries of welcome, she looked less tired but very bedraggled from her long wait and walk in the rain. She gazed around the house admiringly, it looked very well kept somehow. There was much more peace

73

than there had been three weeks ago when, weary and beaten, she had left it.

'I'll only have a very little piece of cake,' she said proudly, 'I've lost nearly a stone.' They all cooed over her, and Derek put his arm protectively around her shoulder and said he was delighted to have her back and her old self.

Dara tactfully went to bed early after dinner to leave them together. Derek began to tell Elizabeth about the new turn in his work but from habit her mind wandered, and she said she must think of tomorrow's lunch.

'It's done,' he said irritably.

'Done? How can it be done?' she asked mystified.

'Well it's Saturday tomorrow darling. We'll be going out shopping early, and then home to soup and sandwiches, like we do every Saturday.'

'Well I'll make the sandwiches, if we're going to leave early,' said Elizabeth, a bit discomfited to hear him say 'like every Saturday', when there had only been three Saturdays.

'Oh, darling. They're made. We always have something on Friday night that can end up as sandwiches next day. Dara has mashed up the chicken with some mayonnaise I expect, and we'll get nice crusty bread tomorrow and that's lunch.' He said it with such confidence and sense of repeating the obvious that Elizabeth felt both amused and yet chilled. How very well the house had managed without her.

'It's a good idea this Saturday shopping then?' she asked timidly.

'Well, it makes sense doesn't it?' said Derek, making nothing of five years of her standing in line at delicatessens and greengrocers during lunch hours and carrying them home on crowded buses.

But the week was sheer pleasure. She went back to work and was oohed and aahed over by the other nurses and by her patients who all praised that nice Irish nurse who had been there during her illness.

Each evening when she got back the house seemed like a welcoming palace; Dara had used the time to do a thorough spring clean and a reorganization of the linen cupboard.

'Can you give me a list of all the things you buy on a Saturday?' Elizabeth asked humbly.

'Could you explain what exactly you do in the garden?' she begged.

'How are the clothes always clean when you are here?' she implored.

Dara always answered helpfully. She never implied that Elizabeth was an incompetent.

The day before she left Elizabeth said, 'I don't think I'm as right as rain.'

'You're nearly as right as rain,' said Dara as they sat in the sparkling kitchen and had a cup of tea. The children were gurgling happily in their bedroom-cum-playroom, and Derek was having a shower before his evening sherry and chat before dinner.

'What'll I do, Dara?' she asked.

'You *could* quit work, take a lodger to make up some of the dough.'

'No, no.'

'You could do extra hours for the agency and employ a home help.'

'No, no,' said Elizabeth.

'Well, just keep sort of going I suppose,' said Dara. 'I mean it's not anyone's fault that you're not as right as rain. It's not Derek's fault, he's smashing, and the kids are lovely, and the work's fine, and that neighbour of yours is a real pal, if you take her kids on a Sunday she'll do anything for you. She loves her Sundays.'

'Don't go,' Elizabeth begged.

'Aw, come on Eliza,' Dara always called her that. For over twenty years it has been 'Come on Eliza'.

Eliza looked at her, hoping for a solution.

'Of course I've got to go. Take it easy, take it nice and easy. There aren't any problems at all you know.'

75

Elizabeth looked at her friend carefully. Dara had said that about Mother and Father. 'Aw, come on Eliza they're only having a bit of a barney with each other . . .' then they had got divorced.

'Aw, come on Eliza, it's not the end of the world, they're both nice happy people, don't make them into old miseries by your own attitude. Enjoy both of them.' Fine until Father had committed suicide and Mother had joined that funny religion of nutters leaving a small legacy to Elizabeth as a gesture towards sanity and family life.

'Aw, come on Eliza, everyone works and runs a home these days – why do you think you're going to be the one who won't manage?' she had said when Elizabeth had first complained of finding it all a little too much.

'Eliza, you'll be as right as rain,' she had said only four weeks ago. And Eliza wasn't.

It had always been the same, when Dara had left, Mother and Father had looked at her and each other, expecting something that Elizabeth wasn't able to give, and being disappointed with her, unreasonably disappointed, because she couldn't. She realized that everyone – Derek, Benny, Nell, that tiresome neighbour, the people at the agency – would all look expectantly at Elizabeth and wish that there was something there, something that Dara's presence had led them to believe was there.

She looked at her friend, and wondered for the first time why she hadn't had a duller friend, one against whom she could be measured and come out winning. Someone dull who would make her shine. Someone messy who would make her seem organized by comparison.

It had been a bad thing to have had Dara to stay. It had been a bad thing for twenty-six years, but she only realized it now, when she was as far as she ever was from being as right as rain.

Warren Street

Nan had had another god-awful day. Nobody seemed to use any under-arm deodorant any more. She had been wincing from whiffs of sweat all day, as people flung off their garments to try on her designs.

That maddening Mrs Fine had, of course, noticed the seam that wasn't exactly right; while that stupid, stupid woman – who apparently worked in some important position in an estate agents – had forgotten again what she wanted made out of the woollen material but was absolutely certain that it wasn't the poncho that Nan had cut out for her.

'Why would I have said a poncho, when I have one already?' she asked wide-eyed.

'That's what I asked you at the time,' hissed Nan.

But the thing that was making Nan's heart leaden was that she had had a row with Shirley.

Now nobody had rows with Shirley. She had a face so like the rising sun you expected rays to stick out from her head like in a child's drawing. If Nan had rowed with her, it had to have been Nan's fault and that was that.

Shirley had been coming to Nan for two years now, ordering maybe five garments a year. Nan remembered the first day she came she had been pressing her nose against the window rather wistfully, looking at a little bolero and skirt outfit on display. The skirt wouldn't have gone over Shirley's head, let alone made it to her waist.

Nan pulled back the curtain and waved her inside –

she still wondered why she did it. Normally she never encouraged customers. She had enough enquiries she couldn't deal with, and this was obviously not a fashion-conscious girl whom it would be a pleasure to dress.

Shirley's great, happy face and bouncing, bulging body arrived in Nan's little shop.

'I think I have the wrong place,' she began. 'Lola who works with me and who's eight months pregnant said she got her smocks here, and I was wondering if you have any more smocks. I mean, they might fit me, even though I'm not pregnant.'

Nan had liked her cheerful face so much she'd encouraged her.

'Sit down. I'll go and see. I've very few things really – I mainly make clothes up for people you see.'

'Oh, are you a designer?' asked Shirley innocently.

She had touched on something very near to Nan's heart. She would have liked to think of herself as a designer and she had a flair for ideas and style. She sold things to classy boutiques from time to time. But something about Shirley's face made her answer, to her own surprise: 'No, more a dressmaker.'

'Oh, that's great,' Shirley had said. 'I thought that they'd disappeared. I wonder, would you be able to make me a smock . . .?' She broke off, seeing a refusal beginning to form itself on Nan's face.

'Oh, please, please do!' she said. 'I can't find anything in the shops that doesn't have white collars or tiny, thoughtful, mum-to-be prints on it.'

'It's just that I'm very busy . . .' Nan began.

'It would be very easy to do,' said Shirley. 'You wouldn't have to put any shape in it, and you wouldn't have to waste time wondering if the fit was right.' She grinned encouragingly, and that did it. Nan couldn't bear her to go around the world as vulnerable as that, and indeed, as badly dressed in that hideous, diagonally-striped garment she had on.

'You win,' Nan had said, and they spent a happy half-hour planning what Shirley would wear for the winter.

Away went the belted grey army issue-type coats – the only one that fitted Shirley – and on came a cape. Away, too, the men's warm sweaters and on with a rosy red dress and a warm pink one.

Nan also made her a multi-coloured evening dress, which had all the shades of the rainbow in it. It was, she thought, a pleasure to design a dress for Shirley. She was so grateful, so touched and happy when it was finished. Sometimes she would whirl around in it in front of the mirror, her fat little hands clasped excitedly like a child.

Shirley was one of the few clients who didn't seem to have a list of complaints and personal problems, which was another bonus. Nan thought of Mrs Fine, always running down her husband. Shirley never complained about men at all.

Miss Harris was always bitching about traffic or work, or how you couldn't get a taxi or a waiter who spoke English, or proper wholemeal bread. Shirley never seemed in the least upset by such deprivations.

In fact, Nan knew little of Shirley's life, except that she fancied her boss in an advertising agency. Or maybe she didn't – Shirley was always so jokey. The last garment she had made Shirley was a really lovely dress. Nan had spent hours on the very fine wool, with its embroidery, ruffs and frills, its soft blues and yellows. Shirley looked like an enormous, beautiful baby.

It was for some gala evening and Shirley had said: 'If he doesn't tear the clothes off me when he sees me like this, he never will.'

Nan worked on a system of appointments that meant you had to come and see her on the hour, and she only saw eight people a day. That way, she said, the job was manageable. People didn't stay longer than twenty minutes at the most. The rest of the hour Nan worked away with her quiet, little machinist burring on in the background.

She would never be rich, never be famous, but it was a living. She couldn't see a life where she would be finishing buttonholes at three a.m. for a show next day. Her own life and her own lover were far too precious for that. Colin and she had lived together happily for ages and often thought of getting married but they'd never actually got the details organized.

That's what they said. The truth was that Colin would have disappeared very sharply if Nan had suggested marriage. She didn't mind much; although sometimes she felt he had it all ways since they both worked. She did the housework and paid the rent; but then it was her place, and he did share the bills.

And he loved the fact that she worked downstairs. Sometimes if he had a day off he would come in and give her a rose in the workroom, and on one never-to-be-forgotten occasion he had asked the machinist to go for a walk, locked the door and made love to her there and then, to the accompaniment of Miss Harris pounding on the door.

One day Colin had seen Shirley leaving with a finished dress. 'Who on earth was the beach ball bouncing out a minute ago?' he asked. Shirley wasn't the usual mould of Nan's clients.

'That's our Shirl whom I talk about sometimes,' Nan said.

'You never told me she looked like a technicoloured Moby Dick,' said Colin. Nan was annoyed. True, Shirley was enormous; true, she was dressed extremely brightly – mainly at Nan's insistence. But because she had such a lovely face, she looked well in colourful clothes and Nan didn't like Colin's joke.

'That's a bit uncalled for, isn't it?' she said sharply. Colin was amazed.

'Sorry to tease her – let me hold out my hand for a

80

smack,' he mocked. 'Yes it was very uncalled for, teacher, nobody called for it at all.'

Nan retorted: 'It's cruel to laugh at somebody's shape.'

'Aw, come on, come on,' said Colin reasonably. 'You're always saying someone's like a car aerial or the Michelin Man or whatever. It was just a remark, just a joke.'

Nan forgave him. 'It's just that I feel, I don't know, a bit protective about her. She's so bloody nice compared with almost anyone who comes in here, and she's literally so soft – in every way. I just feel she'd melt into a little pool if she heard anyone making a remark like that about her, honestly.'

'She was halfway down the street before I opened my mouth,' said Colin.

'I know – I suppose I just hope that nobody says such things whether she hears them or not,' said Nan.

That conversation had been a few months ago, Nan reflected, as she sat, head in hands. Funny that it all came back to her now. She did remember exactly how protective she had felt, as if Shirley had been her favourite sister and their mother had entrusted Nan with the care of seeing that nobody ever laughed at the fat girl.

Nan could hardly believe that, not half an hour ago, Shirley had banged out of the door and shouted from the street that she would never come back. It was like a nightmare where people behave completely out of character.

Shirley had come along for a final fitting for the wedding outfit. Her best friend was getting married and Shirley and Nan had been through reams of ideas before setting on the emerald green dress and matching hat.

Nan had been delighted with it and Shirley's face was a picture of happiness as they both looked at the outfit in the mirror: the tall, slim, slightly wary-looking dressmaker in her elegant grey wool tunic and the short, mountainous client in her metres and metres of glittering emerald.

'You'll need green eye-shadow, not blue,' said Nan. 'I'll lend you some for the wedding if you like.' She looked around for her bag. 'Do you know, I was running out of some, and then I thought of you and this colour, so I asked Colin to get me some. He's in the trade, you know, so it's a little perk. I can't find the wretched thing anywhere.' As she hunted for the parcel which wasn't in her handbag after all, Nan felt a strange, unnatural, silence descend behind her.

'Is that it?' asked Shirley, holding up an envelope that was on a table. The envelope had writing on it. It said 'Green eye-shadow for burly Shirley'.

The two women looked at the inscription in silence for what must have been only four seconds or so, but seemed never-ending. Nan could think of only one thing to say.

When it was obvious that Shirley was going to say nothing either, she tried, but her voice only came out like a squeak. What she had been going to say was, 'I didn't write that', and that didn't seem a very helpful thing to say at that moment.

She thought she would kill Colin. She would physically hurt him and bruise him for this. She would never forgive him.

Shirley's face had turned pink. Her fat neck had gone pink too, which didn't go very well with the emerald.

'Is that what you call me: "Burly Shirley"? Well I suppose it has the advantage of rhyming,' she said. She was so hurt she was almost bleeding.

Nan found her words finally. 'Colin has rude, destructive nicknames for all my clients. It amuses him – it's childish, immature and senseless,' she snapped fiercely.

'How does he know I'm . . . burly? He's never met me,' said Shirley.

'Well, you see he makes up these nicknames without knowing who people are. You do see that it's not an insult and it's not a comment. He could have written anything.' Nan nearly laughed with relief. How marvellous to get out of it in this way. But Shirley was looking at her oddly.

'So I expect he just chose the word because it rhymes with your name. If you had been called Dotty he might have said Spotty.' Nan was very pleased with herself, at the unknown powers of invention that were suddenly welling up within her.

Shirley just looked.

'So now that's cleared up, why don't you take the eye-shadow and put a little on to see how it looks with the outfit?' urged Nan.

Shirley politely started to put it on, and Nan released her breath and foolishly didn't leave well, or nearly well, alone.

'I mean it's not as if anyone would deliberately make a joke about being fat to anyone, not that you are very fat or anything, but one wouldn't mention it even if you were.'

'Why not?' asked Shirley.

'Why? Well, you know why – it would be rude and hurtful to tell someone they were fat. Like saying they were ugly or . . . you know . . .'

'I didn't think being fat was on the same level as being ugly, did you?'

Desperately Nan tried to get back to the comparatively happy level they had just clawed their way to a few moments ago.

'No, of course I don't think being fat is the same as being ugly, but you know what I mean – nobody wants to be either if they can possibly avoid it.'

'I haven't hated being fat,' said Shirley. 'But I wouldn't like to think it was on a par with being ugly – something that would revolt people and make them want to turn away.'

'You're not very fat, Shirley,' Nan cried desperately.

'Oh but I am, I am very fat. I am very short and weigh sixteen stone, and no normal clothes will fit me. I am very, very fat, actually,' said Shirley.

'Yes, but you're not really fat; you're not fat like . . .' Nan's inventive streak gave out and she stopped.

'I'm the fattest person you know, right? Right. I thought it didn't matter so much because I sort of felt I had a pretty face.'

'Well, you do have a very pretty face.'

'You gave me the courage to wear all these bright clothes instead of the blacks and browns . . .'

'You look lovely in . . .'

'And I didn't worry about looking a bit ridiculous; but you know, ridiculous was the worst I thought I ever looked. I didn't think it was ugly . . .'

'It isn't, you misunderstood . . .'

'It's always disappointing when you discover that someone hasn't been sincere, and has just been having a bit of fun, that she's just been pitying you.'

'I don't pity you . . . I wasn't . . .'

'But thanks anyway, for the outfit.' Shirley started to leave. 'It's lovely and I'm really very grateful. But I won't take the eye-shadow, if you don't mind.'

'Shirley will you sit down . . .?'

'The cheque is here – that *is* the right price, by the way? You're not doing it cheaply just for me, I hope.'

'Please, listen . . .'

'No, I'm off now. The life has gone out of it here, now that you pity me. I suppose it's just silly pride on my part, but I wouldn't enjoy it any more.'

'Shirley, let me say something. I regard you as my most valued customer. I know that sounds like something out of a book, but I mean it. I looked forward to your coming here. Compared with most of the others, you're a joy – like a friend, a breath of fresh air. I enjoyed the days that you'd been. Now don't make me go down on my knees. Don't be touchy . . .'

'You've always been very friendly and helpful . . .'

'Friendly . . . helpful . . . I regard you as some kind of kid sister or daughter. I had a fight with Colin about you not three months ago, when he said you looked like Moby Dick with stripes or something.'

'Oh yes.'

'Oh God.'

Shirley had gone. The bang of the door nearly took the pictures off the walls.

'I'll miss her dreadfully,' thought Nan. 'She was the only one with any warmth or life. The rest are just bodies for the clothes.' To hell with it. She would telephone Lola, the friend who had sent Shirley to her in the first place.

'Listen, Lola, this sounds trivial, but you know that nice Shirley who worked with you . . .'

'Shirley Green? Yeah, what about her?'

'No, her name is Kent, Shirley Kent.'

'I know it used to be till she married Alan Green.'

'Married?'

'Nan, do you feel okay? You made her wedding dress for her, about a year ago.'

'She never told me she got married. Who's Alan Green? Her husband?'

'Well, he's my boss, and was hers. Nan, what is this?'

'Why do you think she didn't tell me she got married?'

'Nan, I haven't an idea in the whole wide world why she didn't tell you. Is this what you rang up to ask me?'

'Well have a guess. Think why she mightn't have told me.'

'It might have been because you and Colin weren't getting married. She's very sensitive, old Shirl, and she wouldn't want to let you think she was pitying you or anything.'

'No, I suppose not.'

'Anyway, it was the most smashing wedding dress – all that ruffle stuff and all those lovely blues and lace embroidery. I thought it was the nicest thing you've ever made.'

Oxford Circus

Once she had decided to write the letter, Joy thought that it would be easy. She had never found it difficult to express herself. She found her big box of simple, expensive writing-paper and began with a flourish: 'Dear Linda . . .' and then she came to a sudden stop.

Joy didn't want to use any clichés about Linda being surprised to hear from her, she didn't want to begin by explaining who she was, since Linda knew. She had no wish to start by asking a favour since that would put her in a subservient role, and Joy wanted to have the upper hand in this whole business. She didn't want it to seem like girlish intrigue; both she and Linda were long past the age when schoolgirl plots held any allure.

Eventually she wrote a very short note indeed and regarded it with great pleasure before she put it into the envelope.

Linda,

I'm sure my name is familiar to you from the long distant past when Edward was both your friend and mine. There is something I would very much like to discuss with you, something that has little bearing on the past and certainly nothing to do with either nostalgia or recriminations! Perhaps if you are coming to London in the next few weeks, you could let me know and I can take you to lunch?

Sincerely, Joy Martin.

Linda re-read the letter for the twentieth time. Everything, every single warning bell inside her told her to throw it away, to pretend she had never read it. Joy Martin must be mad to want to reopen all the hurts and deceptions and rivalries of ten years ago. They had never met, but she had read all Joy's passionate letters to Edward, she had sneaked a look at the photographs of Joy and Edward taken on their illicit weekends, the weekends when Edward had said he was visiting his elderly mother. Linda could feel her throat and chest constricting with the remembered humiliations and injustices of a previous decade. Throw it away, burn it. Don't bring it all back. It was destructive then, it can only be destructive again now.

Dear Joy,

How intriguing! I thought this kind of thing only happened in glorious old black and white movies. Yes, I do come to London fairly often and will most certainly take you up on your offer of lunch. Can we make it somewhere near Oxford Circus? That way it will leave me right in the middle of the shopping belt. Simply mystified to know what all this is about.

Regards, Linda Grey.

Joy breathed a great happy sigh. She had been so afraid of rejection. A whole week had passed without acknowledgement, and she had almost given up hoping for the Hampshire postmark. Her first hurdle had been cleared. She knew now that Linda Grey must feel exactly as she did about Edward. She had not been wrong. There had been a huge amount of caring, almost passion, in her love letters to him – those letters which Joy had sneaked from his wallet to read. There had been purpose and serious intent in her threats of sui- cide. No, her fear that Edward might have been forgot-

ten in Linda's cosy Hampshire life was ... unrealistic.
Edward was never forgotten.

Linda came to London the night before this rendez-
vous. In her handbag she had Joy's card with the name
of the restaurant: '... only a few minutes from Oxford
Circus, as you requested.' She checked in at an inex-
pensive hotel and ordered a cup of tea to wash down
her two sleeping pills. A night in London with the possibility of some showdown involving Edward on the
morrow would keep her awake for hours, and she had
no wish to arrive looking flustered. She had made
appointments for hair and facials. She was going to buy
herself some very expensive shoes and a handbag. Joy
Martin could not sit elegantly and pity poor Linda who
had lost Edward all those years ago. Still, she thought
as her body began to relax with the mogadon. Still, Joy
had lost him too. He had left Joy very shortly after he
had left Linda.

She felt very guilty about Hugh. He had been concerned about her visit to London and wanted to come
with her. No, she assured him, just a check-up. She
really thought she needed the little break as much as
the check-up. She begged him not to come. She would
telephone him tomorrow and tell him that she felt perfect and that the doctor had confirmed it. He would be
pleased and relieved. He would arrange to meet her at
the station and take her out to dinner. He was so kind
and good. She didn't know why she was making this
ridiculous pilgrimage to dig up the hate-filled ghost of
Edward.

Joy woke with a headache and a feeling that something
was wrong. Oh God! This was the day. Linda Grey
would be getting on her train somewhere in the countryside telling her mouse-like husband that she was
going to look at some fabrics in Oxford Street, and was
on her way panting with excitement at the very mention

of Edward's name. She made herself a health drink in the blender and a cup of china tea. But the headache didn't lift so she took some pain-killers very much against her will. Joy liked to believe that she didn't need drugs. Drugs were for weak people. Today that belief didn't seem so clear. She also thought that only weak people stayed away from work when they felt a little below par. But today that wasn't a theory that she could substantiate. She telephoned her secretary. No, of course she wasn't seriously ill, just a little below par. Her secretary was alarmed. Crisply Joy gave instructions, meetings to be rearranged, appointments to be cancelled, letters to be written. She would be back tomorrow morning. Perhaps even this afternoon.

She felt alarmed that it was all taking so much out of her. She had planned it so very carefully. She had allowed no emotion, no waverings. It was now absolutely foolproof. Why did her stomach feel like water? Why did she think she couldn't face her job at all during the day. Full of annoyance she put on her smart sheepskin coat and set out for a long healthy walk in Hyde Park.

As she walked she saw people with their dogs. She would have liked to have a dog; she didn't disapprove of people having dogs in London if they gave them enough exercise. When all this business was over, Joy thought to herself, she might get a dog. A beautiful red setter, and she could walk with him for hours in the park on a bright cold morning like this.

It was five to one and Linda was determined not to be early. She gave herself another admiring look in a window. Her hair was splendid. What a pity that nobody in the village at home could do that sort of thing with scissors and a comb. They really only liked you to have rollers and a half-hour under the dryer. Linda smiled at herself with her newly painted lips. She looked in no way like a woman of nearly forty. She supposed that

Joy Martin probably spent days in beauticians. After all, she had a very glamorous job running an art gallery and an art dealing business. Linda had even seen her photograph once talking to a royal person. Facials and expensive handbags would be no treat for Joy.

She forced her feet to go slowly and only when she saw that she was a nice casual six minutes late did she allow herself to enter the restaurant, take two deep breaths and enquire about a table for two booked by Miss Martin.

'You look smashing,' said Joy warmly. 'Really glamorous. Much younger than you did years ago actually. I always think we improve in our thirties really instead of going off.'

'How on earth do you know what I used to look like?' asked Linda settling herself into the corner chair.

'Oh I used to look at the pictures of you in Edward's wallet. Now, will we have **a gin** or would you prefer a sherry?'

'A gin,' gulped Linda.

'What do you think of me? Have I aged or gone off do you think?'

'No, in fact you look very unsophisticated, sort of wind blown and young,' said Linda truthfully. 'I thought you'd be much more studied, obviously groomed, over made-up. A bit like me,' she giggled.

Joy laughed too. 'I expect you went to a beautician's just to impress me. I was so nervous at the thought of meeting you, I've been out walking all morning in the park. That's why I'm so windswept and rosy. Normally I'm never like this.'

Linda smiled, 'Isn't it funny?' she said. 'After all these years, and we both find it very anxious-making and . . . and well . . . disturbing.'

'Yes,' said Joy. 'That's exactly what it is. Disturbing.'

'Then why did you suggest it, I mean if it's going to make us both anxious and act out of character, what's the point?' Linda's face looked troubled.

Joy paused to order two gin and tonics and to tell the waiter that they would like a little time before they made up their minds about the lunch menu.

'Well,' she said, 'I had to. You see I want you to help me. I want you and I together to murder Edward. Seriously. That's what I'm hoping you'll help me to do.'

Most of Linda's omelette aux fines herbes lay untouched. But Joy had managed to eat much of the whole-wheat pizza. Linda had managed one sip of the dry white wine but it had tasted very sour. The longer Joy talked the more Linda realized that she was indeed perfectly serious.

'Well, it stands to reason that he's a man the world would be much better off without. We all agree about that. Well, Linda, be reasonable. There was my divorce. I haven't seen my son for nine and a half years because of Edward. If it hadn't been for Edward I would have a perfectly normal and happy relationship with my son who is now sixteen. As it is I am not allowed to visit him at school; everyone agrees it is less distressing for Anthony if his mother is kept away. Later when he's an adult I shall have some ridiculous "civilized" meeting with him, where we will have nothing to say. So that was one thing Edward destroyed.'

'But you were willing to divorce your husband, to leave everything for Edward. Wasn't it your fault too?'

'No it was not my fault,' Joy was calm and unemotional. 'I was twenty-eight and bored with marriage and a demanding child and Edward lied to me, used me, filled my head with nonsenses, betrayed me and then would not stand by me after I had done what he begged and implored me to do – leave home, leave my husband and child and run away with him. He laughed at me.'

Linda said: 'I didn't know that.'

'And look what he did to you. A nervous breakdown. A serious two-year depression. Two years out of your life because you believed him, and couldn't accept his betrayals, his double life, his endless pointless lies.'

Linda said: 'I didn't think you knew that.'

'There were people before us, Linda, there were people after us. Mine wasn't the only divorce he caused, yours wasn't the only nervous illness. And nobody has punished him. Nobody has said this man is evil and he must be stopped. He mustn't be allowed to roam the world destroying, destroying, turning good to bad and dark, turning simple things to twisted and frightening.' Joy's voice hadn't raised itself a decibel but there was something in it that was a little like a preacher, like some Southern Baptist in a movie describing Satan. It chilled Linda and forced her to speak.

'But it's all over Joy, it's all done. It's all finished. Other people are being silly and foolish nowadays, like you and I once were stupid. They're making mistakes now. Not us.'

Joy interrupted her. 'We were not silly, we made no mistakes, neither do his women of today. We all behaved normally as if Edward were normal. When we said things we meant them. When we told him tales they were true, when we made promises they were sincere.'

Once more her voice was uncomfortably like a preacher. In the busy crowded restaurant Linda felt frightened.

'But you don't seriously want to . . . er . . . get rid of him?'

'Oh yes,' said Joy.

'But why now? Why not years ago, when it hurt more?'

'It hurts just as much now,' said Joy.

'Oh, but it can't', Linda cried sympathetically. 'Not now.'

'Not for myself,' said Joy. 'But now he has gone too far. Now he has done something he can't be forgiven for. He's taken my niece to live with him. She is, of course, utterly besotted with him. She's given up her job for him like you gave up yours, she's given up her fiancé like I gave up my marriage. She will shortly give up her sanity like you did, and her happiness like I did.'

Linda felt a little faint. The smart restaurant seemed somehow claustrophobic.

'Are you very concerned about your niece?' she asked, her voice coming from a long way away. She wanted to keep Joy talking. She didn't want to have to say anything herself.

'Yes, she lives with me. She's all I've got. I've had her since she was seventeen, three years. I thought that if, well if I did a good job looking after her, they might let me have Anthony back too. Anyway, I'm very attached to Barbara, I've told her everything, she's learning the trade in our company, she's studying art history as well. The one thing I couldn't foresee in a city of twelve million people was that she might meet Edward.'

'Does she know? Does he know?' Linda's voice was still weak: there was a coldness in Joy's tone now that terrified her.

'Barbara doesn't know. I've never seen any reason to tell her about my relationship with Edward. And Edward doesn't remember me.'

'What?'

'He came to the house, to my house last month to collect Barbara, she introduced him to me proudly. His eyes rested on me easily. He doesn't remember me, Linda. He has forgotten me.'

Linda was swept by sympathy for the woman ten years previously she would have like to have killed.

'He pretended. It was another ploy. He *can't* have forgotten you. Joy, don't get hurt over it, you know what he was like. He's just trying to wound you. Don't let him.'

'He had forgotten me, Linda. I am certain he has forgotten you too, and Susan or whoever came after us.

I will not let him use Barbara. She took her things last week and has gone to him!'

'She's twenty years of age Joy, these days that's old enough . . .'

'No day is anyone old enough for Edward, or cruel enough,' said Joy. 'Oh, Barbara is sure she is doing the right thing:

"You know how it is, Auntie Joy.

"You were wild once they say, Auntie Joy.

"If you knew how he makes me need him, Auntie Joy." '

Linda looked across the table. 'Don't tell me what you want to do,' she said.

Joy reached for her hand. 'Please, please. It needs two. You know, you understand, you and I were the same age, we went through the same things. We know. No one else can do it.'

'Don't tell me. I don't want to hear,' said Linda.

'We need two. Nobody can ever connect you with it. You can come up to London for a day, just like today, to buy curtains or whatever. It's in two parts. You needn't even look at him I tell you. He'll be unconscious anyway. I shall have given him the tablets first.'

Linda stood up shakily. 'I beg you not to think about it any more. Do something, anything. Go away. Come and stay in the country with me. Just stop planning it.'

'It has been planned. It's all planned. You are to come to my house, I'll leave the key and the gun.'

'I won't listen,' said Linda. 'I can't listen. You don't want to kill him, you want him back. You don't give two damns about your niece. You want Edward. You want him dead if you can't have him. It gives you a wave of pleasure just thinking of his head on one side, dead. His mouth still, his eyes open but not seeing things, not darting . . .'

'How do you know? How can you know that it's like that?' Joy's eyes were bright.

'Because I planned to kill him ten years ago. Ten

94

years ago when you went to live with him. I planned it, too. But I had to plan it on my own. I wasn't confident enough.'

'You what?' Joy looked at her in disbelief.

'I planned it all, I would tell him I needed to see him once. I would assure him there would be no scenes, I would ask him to my flat but in fact I would have some friends there and when he came I would pretend that he had attacked me and that I was fighting him off in self-defence. In the mêlée a knife would be used.'

'Why didn't you do it?' asked Joy.

'Because of you. I knew that you would have known it was murder. You would know Edward didn't care enough for me to attack me. You could have had me convicted.'

'How far had you got?' whispered Joy.

'As far as organizing the knife, the friends in my flat, and asking him to come and see me.'

'And what happened?'

'Oh when he called, I told him I had changed my mind, I didn't want to see him after all. He stayed for one drink, long enough to bewitch Alexandra, my friend.'

'Alex. Oh God! She was your friend?'

'So you saved me from doing it. Let me save you.'

Joy pulled herself together. It was almost a visible thing. First her spine straightened. Then her brow became unlined. A small smile came to her mouth.

'We are being very dramatic, aren't we?' she said in a brittle voice.

'Very,' agreed Linda politely.

'Shall we have coffee, or are you in a hurry to get on with your shopping?'

'Rather a hurry actually,' said Linda.

'So you're off back to Hampshire then and the peaceful life,' said Joy waving for the bill.

'Yes, nothing much to do,' said Linda.

'Very quiet and tranquil I expect,' Joy said producing her credit card for the waiter.

95

'Only excitement I get is reading the papers, seeing who's saying what and doing what. Reading about the things that happen in London, sudden deaths, scandal. You know the kind of thing.'

A small and almost genuine smile came to Joy's eyes.

'I see,' she said.

Linda left, pausing to ask the waiter if there was a phone she could use. She told Hugh that she was very pleased with her check-up and she might catch the earlier train home. He sounded very pleased. And, for the first time in a long time, his pleasure gave her pleasure too.

Green Park

They had both sworn that they would not dress up. They had assured each other that it would be ridiculous to try to compete with Jane after all these years and considering all the money she had. Very immature really to try on fine feathers and glad rags – like children dressing up and playing games. Yet when they met at the station they were almost unrecognizable from their usual selves.

Helen had bought a new hat with a jaunty feather, and Margaret had borrowed a little fur cape. Both of them wore smart shoes and their faces normally innocent of powder had definite evidence of rouge and even eye-shadow. After much mutual recrimination they agreed that they both looked delightful and settled themselves into the train to London with more excitement than two schoolgirls.

How extraordinary to be heading off for tea at the Ritz with Jane. Helen whispered that she would love to tell everybody in the railway compartment that this was where they were heading. Margaret said it would be more fun to let it fall casually in conversation afterwards: 'How nice you look today, Mrs Brown, what a sensible colour to wear, lots of people in the Ritz last week seemed to be wearing it.'

And of course they giggled all the more because, in spite of sending themselves up, they actually were a little nervous about going to somewhere as splendid as the Ritz. They were over-awed. The very mention of the Ritz made them nervous. It was for perfumed, furred people not people who had dabbed some of last Christmas's perfume behind the ears and borrowed a sister-in-law's well-worn Indian lamb.

In some way both Helen and Margaret feared they might be unmasked when they got there. And they giggled and joked all the more to stifle this fear.

None of their fear was directed towards Jane. Jane was one of their own. Jane had trained to be a children's nanny with them all those years ago. You don't forget the friends made during that kind of apprenticeship. It was far more binding than the services were for 'men. It was almost like having survived a shipwreck – the eighteen girls who survived that particular obstacle race in the school for nannies, which had long since closed down, had forged a friendship which would last for life. Some of them had gone to the Gulf states and they wrote regular newsletters saying how they were getting on. Some, like Helen and Margaret, had married and applied their nanny training to their own children; only Jane had become spectacular and famous. But because she was Jane from the nanny training school it didn't matter if she became head of the United Nations, Helen and Margaret would never be in awe of her.

They changed trains, twittering happily at Euston and took the underground to Green Park.

'Perhaps people think we are career women, dropping into the Ritz for a business conference,' whispered Helen.

'Or wealthy wives up for a day's shopping,' sighed Margaret.

Neither Margaret nor Helen were wealthy. Margaret was actually married to a vicar and lived in a draughty vicarage. She was so much the vicar's wife now that she felt quite guilty about wearing the Indian lamb in case any of her husband's parishioners saw her and wondered about her showiness. Helen, too, was far from wealthy. Jeff, her husband, had a flair for backing things that went wrong and that included horses. Yet never had a hint of envy been spoken or indeed felt by the two women about the wealthy friend they were en route to meet.

Jane was the mistress of a very eccentric and extraordinarily wealthy American industrialist. He had bought her many gifts, including a ranch and a small television station; she was one of the world's richest and best known kept women.

For the twentieth time Margaret wondered if Jane could possibly look as well as she appeared in the photographs, and for the twentieth time Helen said it was quite possible. If you didn't have to do anything each day except make yourself look well, then it was obvious you could look magnificent. Suppose each day when Margaret got up she didn't have to clean the vicarage, take her children to school, shop, cook, wash, go to coffee mornings, sales of work, cookery demonstrations and entertain the doctor, the curate, the headmaster – think how well she could look. Margaret had a very good bone structure, Helen agreed grudgingly, she could look very striking if only she had time to lavish on herself. Margaret felt a bit depressed by this; she knew that Helen meant it as a compliment but it left her feeling as if she were in fact a great mess because she didn't have this time, and that her good bone structure was wasted.

As they came up from Green Park tube station into the sunlight of Piccadilly the two women giggled again and reached for their powder compacts before they crossed the road to the Ritz.

'Aren't we silly?' tittered Helen. 'I mean we're forty years of age.'

'Yes, so is Jane of course,' said Margaret as if that was some kind of steadying fact. Something that would keep their feet on the ground.

Jane had been attractive twenty years ago, but she was a beauty now.

'You look ridiculous,' gasped Helen. 'Your face, your whole face, it's the face of a twenty year old. You look better than when we were all teenagers.'

Jane gave a great laugh showing all her perfect teeth.

'Aw, for Christ's sake Helen, I bought this face, and bloody boring it was, I tell you. It's easy to have a face like that. Just give it to someone else to massage it and pummel it and file the teeth down and put caps on, no the face isn't any problem.'

Margaret felt that she wished the foyer of this over-powering hotel would open and gulp her into the basement area. She had never felt so foolish, in her ratty overdressed, over-done bit of Indian lamb.

'Come on, we'll go to the suite,' Jane said, an arm around each of their shoulders. She noticed how impressed Helen and Margaret were with the tea lounge and the pillars and the little arm chairs beside little tables where only the very confident could sit waiting casually for their friends. She knew they would love to sit in the public area and drink it all in with Jane herself there to protect them.

'We'll come back and do the grand tour later, but now we go and meet Charles.'

'Charles?' Both women said it together with the alarm that might be generated at a dorm feast if someone mentioned that the headmistress was on her way. It was obvious that neither of them had thought that the ordeal of meeting Charles was included in the invitation to tea.

'Oh yeah, the old bat wants to make sure I really am meeting two old chums from the college. He has a fear, you see, that I'll have hired two male go-go dancers from some show. I want him to get a look at you so that he can see you are the genuine article, not something I made up. Come on, we'll get it over with, and then we can settle down to cream cakes and tea and gins and tonics.'

Because Jane had shepherded them so expertly

towards the lift, Margaret and Helen hadn't even had time to exchange a glance until they found themselves outside a door where two tall men stood.

'Are they bodyguards?' whispered Margaret.

'They speak English,' laughed Jane. 'I know they look like waxworks, but that's part of the qualifications. If you came in here with a machine-gun to kill Charles you wouldn't get far.'

They were nodded in by the unsmiling heavies at the door, and Charles was visible. He stood by the window looking out at the traffic below. A small, old, worried man. He looked a bit like her father-in-law, Helen thought suddenly. A fussy little man in an old people's home who didn't really care when she and Jeff went to see him, he only cared about what time it was, and was constantly checking his watch with clocks.

When Charles did give them his attention he had a wonderful smile. It was all over his face, even his nose and chin seemed to be smiling. Margaret and Helen stopped being nervous.

'I'm a foolish old gentleman,' he said in a Southern States drawl. 'I'm jes' so nervous of my Jane, I always want to see who she goes out with.'

'Heavens,' said Margaret.

'Well, I see, how nice,' stammered Helen.

'You ladies jes' must understand me. I guess you know how it is when you only live with someone, you aren't so sure, its not the same binding thing as marriage,' he looked at them winningly, expecting some support.

Margaret found her vicar's wife's voice: 'Honestly, Mr ... er ... Charles ... I'm not in any position to know what you're talking about. I don't know any couples who live together who are not married.'

She couldn't in a million years have said anything more suitable. Jane's mouth had a flicker of a smile and in two minutes Charles had taken his briefcase, his personal assistant, and his bodyguards and having made charming excuses he left for a meeting that had been delayed presumably until he had satisfied himself about Jane's activities and plans for the afternoon.

'Is the place bugged?' Helen whispered fearfully when he had gone. Her eyes were like big blue and white china plates.

Jane screamed with laughter: 'Darling Helen, no of course not. Hey, I'm really very sorry for putting all that on you both but you see the way he is.'

'Very jealous?' suggested Helen, still in a low voice.

'A little paranoid?' Margaret offered.

'No, dying actually,' said Jane flatly, and went to get a jewelled cigarette box. 'Yeah, he only has two months, poor old bat. He's half the size he was six months ago. They said well under a year, now it's getting quicker.'

She sounded as if she were talking about a tragedy in some distant land, a happening in a country where she had never been. Everyone is sad about far floods and droughts but they don't concern people like near ones do. Jane spoke of Charles as if he were a figure she had read about in a Sunday paper, not a man she had lived with for ten years. She seemed neither upset nor relieved by his terminal illness, it was just one of the many sad things that happen in life.

'I'm very sorry,' said Margaret conventionally.

'He doesn't look as if he had only a short time to live,' said Helen.

'I'm sure that if he's not going to get better it's all for the best that it should happen swiftly,' said Margaret being a vicar's wife again.

'Aw shit, that's not what I wanted to see you about,' said Jane. She looked at their shocked faces.

'Look, sorry, sorry for the language, and this, well, lack of feeling. I *am* sorry for the old bastard, he's been very brave, and he's very frightened, you know. But hell, Margaret, Helen, we are not fools. I mean, be straight. He's hardly the love of my life.'

There was a silence. Whatever they had expected from afternoon tea with Jane in the Ritz, it certainly was not this.

Jane appealed to them: 'I thought that being in the nanny school was blood brothers, you know, for life? I thought that those of us who survived could say anything, anything and it wasn't misconstrued.'

Margaret said: 'Jane, of course you can say anything to me but remember we've all lived a life since we came out of nanny school. Mine has been very sheltered. I'm a vicar's wife for heaven's sake. What can be more sheltered than that? I ask you. It's the kind of thing people make jokes about, it's so, well, so different from yours. Can you really expect me to take all this in my stride?'

'All what?' Jane wanted to know.

'Well your wealth, your lifestyle, the fact that your husband, your common-law husband is dying of cancer and you say awful words and . . .' Margaret looked genuinely distressed. Helen took up the explanation.

'You see, Jane, its not that either Margaret or I are trying to be distant. Its just that we don't really live in the same world as you any more and I expect after a few minutes or an hour we'll all settle down and be the same as we used to be. It's just hard to expect us to act on your level.'

Jane walked around the room for a moment or two before she replied:

'I guess I was taking things a bit too much for granted. I guess I was reading too much into all that solidarity we had twenty years ago.'

She was silent, and looked perplexed. She looked young, beautiful and puzzled, the two matrons stared up at her from their sofa in disbelief. It was if they were watching a film of their youth where only Jane had stayed young. She used to look just like that when she was nineteen and thinking of a way to avoid detection by the nanny college principal.

'You needn't think the friendship isn't there,' said Helen. 'In fact it is, enormously. I can tell Margaret things about my private life, my worries with Jeff and money. Susie was back from Kuwait and when we met she was telling us all about how she discovered she was lesbian and she could tell nobody.' Helen looked like a big innocent schoolgirl trying to join the senior girls by revealing secrets and showing herself to be mature.

'Oh I know, Susie wrote to me,' said Jane absently.

'I feel we've let you down, Jane,' said Margaret. 'I feel there was something you wanted us to do for you, and just by racing the wrong way at the outset we've made that impossible.'

Jane sat down.

'You were always very astute Margaret,' she said. 'There was indeed something I wanted to ask you. But now I don't know whether or not I can. You see I can only do it if I am utterly frank with you. I can't go through any charade with anyone from nanny college. There are rules I break in life but never that.' She looked at them.

'Of course,' said Helen.

'Naturally,' said Margaret.

'Well, you see, I wanted to stay in England until Charles kicks it. No, sorry, if we are going to be frank, I simply will not use words like "passes away", he's dying, he's riddled with cancer, he's not going to see Christmas. I don't wish him any more pain, I wish he were dead. Dead now.'

Their faces were sad, less shocked than before but still not understanding.

'So if we stay here till the end, I want Charles to see that I have friends, good decent normal friends like you two. I want to take him to your homes. He'll probably insult you and buy you new homes but we can get over that. I mean he'll buy you and David a new parsonage certainly Margaret, possibly the bishop's palace, and as for Jeff he'll either buy him a bookmaking business or

104

he'll send him to a Harley Street specialist to have what he will consider compulsive gambling cured in some clinic at three hundred quid a day.'

There was a ghost of a smile passing over the faces of the two on the sofa.

'I wanted to ask your support in these last weeks. There's nobody else I could trust, and I've worked so goddamn hard for ten years I can't lose it all now.'

'What will you lose?' Margaret asked. 'You've already said you won't miss him. I don't see how our inviting him to our homes can help anything at all.'

'Don't you see?' Jane cried out. 'He is going mad, he has premature senility, he's paranoid. He thinks I'm unfaithful to him, he thinks I'm cheating on him. He's busy trying to dispossess me of everything.'

'He can't do that,' Helen gasped.

'You can't think that,' Margaret gasped at the same time.

'He can, he can do a lot of it, and I can and do think it because I know it,' said Jane.

In simple terms she told them a tale of stocks and companies, of the properties she owned absolutely which could not be repossessed, of the shares that had been bought back. The two women sat mutely listening to companies which were merged and stock transferred. They heard of the invalid wife whom Charles would never divorce because in his part of Georgia only cads and men who were not gentlemen divorced invalids. They heard of his suspicions, none of them founded on any truth, that Jane was in fact using his riches to buy herself young lovers.

'Even so, even if he does dispossess you,' said Helen, trying to find a word of consolation, 'You'll still be very rich.'

Margaret thought of the corridors upstairs in the vicarage which would never have a carpet on them because they could only afford to carpet to the top of the stairs.

'You'll still be young Jane, and wealthy compared to almost everyone,' she said. 'I can't see how anything will be so terrible.'

'It's terrible to be denied over ninety per cent of what I could have had,' said Jane. 'If the old bat had stayed sane. That's why I want to try and recoup as much as I can. I can't chain him to his bed. The lawyers for his various trusts are slobbering with greed. They're helping him each bloody hour to get more away from me. My lawyers say it's an unequal struggle. They even want to be paid in advance in case I'm left with nothing at the end.'

She looked like a thwarted child.

'How would coming to visit us help?' Helen asked trembling at the thought of bodyguards and Charles and huge cars in her small terraced house.

'He'd see I was normal, came from some normal sinless background. He's heavily into sin now that he can't commit any any more. He'd see heavy respectability in your homes. We could act out a pantomime till he snuffs it.'

Margaret gave her a look of great distaste.

'You can't mean it, Jane.'

'I do.'

Helen looked at her as if she had been someone apologising for a drunken scene.

'You can't have been aware of what you were asking us to do. That's why you feel you can no longer ask it,' she said.

Jane looked at them slowly.

'I'm asking you to join in a little deception with me, I'm telling you the whole score, I'm explaining why, and why I need it.'

'But Jane, it's so dishonest, it's so phoney, so high-powered,' said Margaret.

'I think it's only because you imagine it's *high-powered* you're asking me to drop it,' said Jane. 'We went in for a lot of things that were phoney and dishonest in the old days. No holds were barred when you two were landing your men but now that we're older and the stakes are higher, it's high-powered as well as dishonest, we can't do it.'

With a very swift movement she lifted a telephone and cancelled afternoon tea asking room service to make sure it was set for them downstairs instead.

'My guests will prefer to eat in the tea lounge instead,' she said crisply.

Her eyes were bright, she dismissed any further discussion of the matter, she shepherded them neatly downstairs, past another bodyguard at the door who plodded discreetly after them and eventually positioned himself in the hotel lobby where he could see them at all times.

As she poured tea, Jane insisted on hearing of all their happenings, and little by little the guard relaxed sufficiently for them to talk about their homes and lives. She told them, too, about some of the things she had done. Nothing relating to Charles and his short future or his pathetic paranoia.

She told how she had met a famous film star, and she described what it was like to have a beautician arrive every morning at seven a.m. and not to allow you to face the world until after nine. She ate no cream cakes but urged the others to finish the plate.

They parted at the door under the admiring glance of many people who thought Jane quite startlingly attractive, and under the watchful glance of the bodyguard who had instructions not to let Jane out of his sight. There were little kisses and assurances of further letters and visits and meetings, there were clasps and grins and pronouncements that it would all turn out fine in the end.

Helen and Margaret went down into the tube again. Green Park station looked less full of promise and giggles and a day out.

'Everything they say about money not bringing happiness is true,' said Helen as she fumbled in her shabby purse for the coins for her ticket.

'You would have thought that with all that money and high life she would have been contented, but no, it's more, ever searching for more,' said Margaret.

They were very silent going home. It was unlike them to be silent. Such a long friendship meant that they could say things which others wouldn't broach. But even the apprenticeship in the nanny college and all that it involved was no help to them now.

Helen thought about how Jane had helped her to raise the money for her wedding to Jeff, when Jeff had lost the whole three hundred pounds on a horse. Jane had been efficient and practical and dishonest. She had sold tickets for a charity that did not exist. She delivered the money to Helen without a comment.

Margaret was thinking of the early days when she had fallen for Dave, the handsome divinity student. Jane had helped her then, so well had Jane helped her that David's fiancée had been dislodged. There was just a rumour here and tittle tattle there so that poor David thought that he had become engaged to a Jezebel. While the same process in reverse was worked about Margaret. A blameless innocent was how Margaret appeared.

In those days it had seemed the normal thing to do, to support your friends. After all, everyone knew that men were notoriously difficult and could cause all kinds of hurtful problems. They were always misunderstanding things. It was only right that friends should help each other when there was a problem of that sort. Those were their thoughts, but they didn't share them.

Victoria

Rose looked at the woman with the two cardboard cups of coffee. She had one of those good-natured faces that you always associate with good works. Rose had seen smiles like that selling jam at fêtes or bending over beds on hospitals or holding out collecting boxes hopefully.

And indeed the woman and the coffee headed for an old man wrapped up well in a thick overcoat even though the weather was warm, and the crowded coffee bar in Victoria Station was even warmer.

'I think we should drink it fairly quickly, Dad,' said the woman in a half-laughing way. 'I read somewhere that if you leave it for any length at all, the cardboard melts into the coffee and that's why it tastes so terrible.'

He drank it up obediently and he said it wasn't at all bad. He had a nice smile. Suddenly, and for no reason, he reminded Rose of her own father. The good-natured woman gave the old man a paper and his magnifying glass and told him not to worry about the time, she'd keep an eye on the clock and have them on the platform miles ahead of the departure time. Secure and happy he read the paper and the good-natured woman read her own. Rose thought they looked very nice and contented and felt cheered to see a good scene in a café instead of all those depressing, gloomy scenes you can see, like middle-aged couples staring into space and having nothing to say to each other.

She looked at the labels on their suitcases. They were heading for Amsterdam. The name of the hotel had been neatly typed. The suitcases had little wheels under them. Rose felt this woman was one of the world's good and wise organizers. Nothing was left to chance, it would be a very well-planned little holiday.

The woman had a plain wedding ring on. She might be a widow. Her husband might have left her for someone outrageous and bad-natured. Her husband and four children might all be at home and this woman was just taking her father to Amsterdam because he had seemed in poor spirits. Rose made up a lot of explanations and finally decided that the woman's husband had been killed in an appalling accident which she had borne very bravely and she now worked for a local charity and that she and her father went on a holiday to a different European capital every year.

Had the snack bar been more comfortable she might have talked to them. They were not the kind of people to brush away a pleasant conversational opening. But it would have meant moving all her luggage nearer to them, it seemed a lot of fuss. Leave them alone. Let them read their papers, let the woman glance at the clock occasionally, and eventually let them leave. Quietly, without rushing, without fuss. Everything neatly stowed in the two bags on wheels. Slowly, sedately, they moved towards a train for the south coast. Rose was sorry to see them go. Four German students took their place. Young, strong and blond, spreading German and English coins out on the table and working out how much they could buy between them. They didn't seem so real.

There was something *reassuring* she thought about being able to go on a holiday with your father. It was like saying, thank you, it was like stating that it had all been worthwhile, all that business of his getting married years ago and begetting you and saving for your future and having hopes for you. It seemed a nice way of rounding things off to be able to take your father to see foreign cities because things had changed so much from his day. Nowadays, young people could manage these things as a matter of course; in your father's day it was still an adventure and a risk to go abroad.

She wondered what her father would say if she set up a trip for him. She wondered only briefly, because really she knew. He'd say, 'No, Rose, my dear, you're very thoughtful but you can't teach an old dog new tricks.'

And she would say that it wasn't a question of that. He wasn't an old dog. He was only barely sixty, and they weren't new tricks, since he used to go to Paris every year when he was a young man, and he and Mum had spent their honeymoon there.

Then he would say that he had such a lot of work to catch up on, so it would be impossible to get away, and if she pointed out that he didn't really have to catch up on anything, that he couldn't have to catch up on anything because he stayed so late at the bank each evening catching up anyway – well, then he would say that he had seen Europe at its best, when it was glorious, and perhaps he shouldn't go back now.

But he'd love to go back, he would love it. Rose knew that. He still had all the scrapbooks and pictures of Paris just before the war. She had grown up with those brown books, and sepia pictures, and menus and advertisements, and maps carefully plotted out, lines of dots and arrows to show which way they had walked to Montmartre and which way they had walked back. He couldn't speak French well, her father, but he knew a few phrases, and he liked the whole style of things French, and used to say they were a very civilized race.

The good-natured woman and her father were probably pulling out of the station by now. Perhaps they were pointing out things to each other as the train gathered speed. A wave of jealousy came over Rose. Why was this woman, an ordinary woman perhaps ten years older than Rose, maybe not even that, why was she able to talk to her father and tell him things and go

111

places with him and type out labels and order meals and take pictures? Why could she do all that and Rose's father wouldn't move from his deck-chair in the sun lounge when his three weeks' holiday period came up? And in his one week in the winter, he caught up on his reading.

Why had a nice, good, warm man like her father got nothing to do, and nowhere to go after all he had done for Rose and for everyone? Tears of rage on his behalf pricked Rose's eyes.

Rose remembered the first time she had been to Paris, and how Daddy had been so interested, and fascinated and dragging out the names of hotels in case she was stuck, and giving her hints on how to get to them. She had been so impatient at twenty, so intolerant, so embarrassed that he thought that things were all like they had been in his day. She had barely listened, she was anxious for his trip down the scrapbooks and up the maps to be over. She had been furious to have had to carry all his carefully transcribed notes. She had never looked at them while there. But that was twenty and perhaps everyone knows how restless everyone else is at twenty and hopefully forgives them a bit. Now at thirty she had been to Paris several times, and because she was much less restless she had found time to visit some of her father's old haunts – dull, merging into their own backgrounds – those that still existed – she was generous enough these days to have photographed them and he spent happy hours examining the new prints and comparing them with the old with clucks of amazement and shakings of the head that the old bakery had gone, or the tree-lined street was now an underpass with six lanes of traffic.

And when Mum was alive she too had looked at the cuttings and exclaimed a bit, and shown interest that was not a real interest. It was only the interest that came from wanting to make Daddy happy.

And after Mum died people had often brought up the

subject to Daddy of his going away. Not too soon after the funeral of course, but months later when one of his old friends from other branches of the bank might call.

'You might think of taking a trip abroad again sometime,' they would say. 'Remember all those places you saw in France? No harm to have a look at them again. Nice little trip.' And Daddy would always smile a bit wistfully. He was so goddamn gentle and unpushy, thought Rose, with another prickle of tears. He didn't push at the bank which was why he wasn't a manager. He hadn't pushed at the neighbours when they built all around and almost over his nice garden, his pride and joy, which was why he was now overlooked by dozens of bed-sitters. He hadn't pushed Rose when Rose said she was going to marry Gus. If only Daddy had been more pushing then, it might have worked. Suppose Daddy had been strong and firm and said that Gus was what they called a bounder in his time and possibly a playboy in present times. Just suppose Daddy had said that. Might she have listened at all or would it have strengthened her resolve to marry the Bad Egg? Maybe those words from Daddy's lips might have brought her up short for a moment, enough to think. Enough to spare her the two years of sadness in marriage and the two more years organizing the divorce.

But Daddy had said nothing. He had said that whatever she thought must be right. He had wished her well, and given them a wedding present for which he must have had to cash in an insurance policy. Gus had been barely appreciative. Gus had been bored with Daddy. Daddy had been unfailingly polite and gentle with Gus. With Gus long gone, Rose had gone back to live in Daddy's house. It was peaceful despite the blocks of bed-sitters. It was undemanding. Daddy kept his little study where he caught up on things, and he always washed saucepans after himself if he had made his own supper. They didn't often eat together. Rose had irregular hours as a traveller and Daddy was so used to reading at his supper, and he ate so early in the evening. If she stayed out at night there were no explanations and no questions. If she told him some of her adventures there was always his pleased interest.

Rose was going to Paris this morning. She had been asked to collect some samples of catalogues. It was a job that might take a week if she were to do it properly or a day if she took a taxi and the first fifty catalogues that caught her eye. She had told Daddy about it this morning. He was interested, and he took out his books to see again what direction the new airport was in, and which areas Rose's bus would pass as she came in to the city centre. He spent a happy half-hour on this, and Rose had looked with both affection and interest. It was ridiculous that he didn't go again. Why didn't he?

Suddenly she thought she knew. She realized it was all because he had nobody to go with. He was, in fact, a timid man. He was a man who said sorry when other people stepped on him, which is what the nicer half of the world does, but it's also sometimes an indication that people might be wary and uneasy about setting up a lonely journey, a strange pilgrimage of return. Rose thought of the good-natured woman and the man who must be ten or fifteen years older than Daddy, tonight they would be eating a meal in a Dutch restaurant. Tonight Daddy would be having his scrambled egg and dead-heading a few roses, while his daughter, Rose, would be yawning at a French restaurant trying not to look as if she were returning the smiles of an ageing lecher. *Why* wasn't Daddy going with her? It was her own stupid fault. All those years, seven of them since Mum had died, seven years, perhaps thirty trips abroad for her, not a mention of inviting Daddy. The woman with the good-natured countenance didn't live in ivory towers of selfishness like that.

Almost knocking over the table, she stumbled out and got a taxi home. He was actually in a cardigan in the garden scratching his head and sucking on his pipe and looking like a stage representation of someone's gentle, amiable father. He was alarmed to see her. He had to be reassured. But why had she changed her mind? Why did it not matter whether she went today or tomorrow? He was worried. Rose didn't do sudden things. Rose did measured things, like he did. Was she positive she was telling him the truth and that she hadn't felt sick or faint or worried?

They were not a father and daughter who hugged and kissed. Pats were more the style of their touching. Rose would pat him on the shoulder and say: 'I'm off now, Daddy,' or he would welcome her home clasping her hand and patting the other arm enthusiastically. His concern as he stood worried among his garden things was almost too much to bear.

'Come in and we'll have a cup of tea, Daddy,' she said, wanting a few moments bent over kettle, sink, tea caddy to right her eyes.

He was a shuffle behind her, anxiety and care in every step. Not wishing to be too inquisitive, not wanting, but plans changed meant bad news. He hated it.

'You're not *doing* anything really, Daddy, on your holidays, are you?' she said eventually, once she could fuss over tea things no longer. He was even more alarmed.

'Rose, my dear, do you have to go to hospital or anything? Rose, my dear, is something wrong? I'd much prefer it if you told me.' Gentle eyes, his lower lip fastened in by his teeth in worry. Oh what a strange father. Who else had never had a row with a father? Was there any other father in the world so willing to praise the good, rejoice in the cheerful, and to forget the bad and the painful?

'Nothing, Daddy, nothing. But I was thinking, it's silly my going to Paris on my own. Staying in a hotel and reading a book and you staying here reading a book or the paper. I was thinking wouldn't it be nice, if I left it until tomorrow and we *both* went. The same way, the way I go by train to Gatwick, or we could get the train to the coast and go by ferry.'

He looked at her, cup halfway to his mouth. He held it there.

'But why, Rose dear? Why do you suggest this?' His face had rarely seemed more troubled. It was as if she had asked him to leave the planet.

'Daddy, you often talk about Paris, you tell *me* about it. I tell *you* about it. Why don't we go together and tell each other about it when we come back?' She looked at him; he was so bewildered she wanted to shout at him, she wanted to finish her sentences through a loud speaker.

Why did he look so unwilling to join? He was being asked to play. Now don't let him hang back, slow to accept like a shy schoolboy who can't believe he has been picked for the team.

'Daddy, it would be nice. We could go out and have a meal and we could go up and walk to Montmartre by the same routes as you took in the Good Old Days. We could do the things you did when you were a wild teen-ager.'

He looked at her frightened, trapped. He was so desperately kind, he saw the need in her. He didn't know how he was going to fight her off. She knew that if she were to get him to come, she must stress that she really wanted it for her, more than for him.

'Daddy, I'm often very lonely when I go to Paris. Often at night particularly I remember that you used to tell me how all of you . . .'

She stopped. He looked like a hunted animal.

'Wouldn't you like to come?' she said in a much calmer voice.

'My dear Rose. *Some time,* I'd love to go to Paris, my dear, there's nothing in the world I'd like to do more than to come to Paris. But I can't go just like that. I can't drop everything and rush off to Paris, my dear. You know that.'

116

'Why not, Daddy?' she begged. She knew she was doing something dangerous, she was spelling out her own flightiness, her own whim of doubling back from the station, she was defining herself as less than level-headed.

She was challenging him, too. She was asking him to say why he couldn't come for a few days of shared foreign things. If he had no explanation, then he was telling her that he was just someone who said he wanted something but didn't reach for it. She could be changing the nature of his little dreams. How would he ever take out his pathetically detailed maps and scrap-books to pore once more with her over routes, and happenings if he had thrown away a chance to see them in three dimensions?

'You have nothing planned, Daddy. It's ideal. We can pack for you. I'll ask them next door to keep an eye on the house. We'll stop the milk and the newspaper and, Daddy, that's it. Tomorrow evening in Paris, tomorrow afternoon we'll be taking that route in together, the one we talked about for me this morning.'

'But Rose, all the things here, my dear, I can't just drop everything. You do see that.'

Twice now he had talked about all the things here that he had to drop. There was *nothing* to drop. What he would drop was pottering about scratching his head about leaf curl. Oh Daddy, don't you see that's all you'll drop? But if you don't see and I tell you, it means I'm telling you that your life is meaningless and futile and pottering. I will not tell *you*, who walked around the house cradling me when I was a crying baby, you who paid for elocution lessons so that I could speak well, you Daddy who paid for that wedding lunch that Gus thought was shabby, you Daddy who smiled and raised your champagne glass to me and said: 'Your mother would have loved this day. A daughter's wedding is a milestone.' I won't tell you that your life is nothing.

117

The good-natured woman and her father were probably at Folkestone or Dover or Newhaven when Rose said to her father that of course he was right, and it had just been a mad idea, but naturally they would plan it for later. Yes, they really must, and when she came back this time they would talk about it seriously, and possibly next summer.

'Or even when I retire,' said Rose's father, the colour coming back into his cheeks. 'When I retire I'll have lots of time to think about these things and plan them.'

'That's a good idea, Daddy,' said Rose. 'I think that's a very good idea. We should think of it for when you retire.'

He began to smile. Reprieve. Rescue. Hope.

'We won't make any definite plans, but we'll always have it there, as something we must talk about doing. Yes, much more sensible,' she said.

'Do you really mean that, Rose? I certainly think it's a good idea,' he said, anxiously raking her face for approval.

'Oh, honestly, Daddy. I think it makes *much* more sense,' she said, wondering why so many loving things had to be lies.

Pimlico

Olive sat in her little office making her weekly lists. First she balanced her books. It didn't take long. Her guests paid weekly and usually by banker's order. Her staff bills were the same every week. The laundry was always precisely the same – thirty-two sheets, thirty-two pillow-cases, thirty-two towels, seven large table-cloths, seven smaller teacloths. Olive had costed the business of getting a washing machine and a dryer and in the end decided that the effort, the space, and the uncertainty in case of breakdowns were simply not worth it. Her food bills were fairly unchanging too; she hadn't been twenty years in the hotel business for nothing. And other bills were simple as well, she transferred a regular amount weekly to meet the electricity, telephone, gas, rates and insurance demands when they arrived. Olive could never understand why other people got into such muddles about money.

Then she made her list of activities for the noticeboard. This involved going through the local papers, the brochures from musical societies and theatres, appeals from charitable organizations for support for jumble sales. When she had a good selection, she would pin them up on her cork board and remove those which had become out of date. She took care to include some items that none of her guests would dream of choosing like Wagner's Ring or a debate about philosophy. But she knew that they liked to be thought the kind of people who might want to patronize such things and it flattered them.

Then she would take out her loose-leaf file, the one she had divided into twelve sections, one for each guest, and in her neat small handwriting Olive would make some small entries under each name. It was here that she felt she could find the heart of her hotel, the memory, the nerve centre. Because Olive knew that the reason her twelve guests stayed with her, was not the great comfort, the food, the value, the style; it was simply because she knew all about them, she remembered their birthdays, their favourite films, their collar sizes, the names of their old homes or native villages. Olive could tell you quite easily the day that Hugh O'Connor had come to live there, all she had to do was open Hugh's section in the file. But it warmed him so much to hear her say: 'Oh, Hugh, don't I remember well the day you arrived, it was a Wednesday in November and you looked very tired.' Hugh would beam to think that he was so important that his arrival had seared itself into Olive's mind.

She never saw anything dishonest or devious about this. She thought it was in fact a common courtesy and a piece of good sense in what people nowadays called 'communications and relating'. In a way it was almost a form of social service. After all, if she was going to go and spend a half-hour with Annie Lynch on a Saturday afternoon, with Annie retired to her bedroom with what looked like the beginnings of a depression, then Olive thought how much more considerate to look up Annie's file and remember the little farm in Mayo and how it had to be sold when Daddy took to the drink, and how Annie's mother who was a walking saint had died and the boys were all married and the only sensible thing for Annie to do was to come and work in London. Olive had filed the kind of things that seemed to cheer Annie up, and would trot them out one by one. Yes, perhaps she should remember everything without writing it down, but really she lived such a busy life. It would be impossible to manage without her little Lists.

Nobody knew of Olive's filing system; they weren't even aware that she seemed to have a better than average memory. Each one of her guests simply marvelled at his or her own good fortune at having found a woman who ran such a comfortable place and who obviously understood them so well. Even the three Spaniards who had been with Olive for five years thought this too. They didn't question their money or their small living quarters, they just appreciated that she could remember their names and their friends' names and the village in the south of Spain where they went back once a year when Olive closed for her two-week break. She was determined that nobody would ever know and had even made preparations that after her death her executor should arrange to have her private records of her years in the hotel business destroyed unread. A solicitor had told her that such a request was perfectly in order.

She was only thirty years of age when she bought the small and then rather seedy hotel in Pimlico. Everyone had assured her that she was quite mad, and that if clever boys who knew about making money hadn't made a go of it, how could an innocent Irish girl with ten years' experience working in a seaside Irish boarding-house hope to do any better? But Olive was determined; she had saved since her teens for the dream of a hotel of her own, and when her uncle's legacy made it actually within her reach she acted at once. Her family in Ireland were outraged.

'There's more to it than meets the eye,' said her mother who foresaw gloomy summers without Olive's considerable help in the boarding-house.

'Maybe she'll find a fellow in London, she hasn't found one here,' said her sister cattily.

Olive's father was enthusiastic that she should try working in London for a little bit before actually committing herself to the buying of a hotel. He had worked there himself for ten years and found it a lonely place.

'When you've seen Piccadilly Circus and Buckingham Palace and you've said to yourself, this is me here sitting listening to Big Ben strike, well that's it. You've seen it then. It's time to come home. It's a scaldingly lonely place.'

As determined as any young woman about to enter religious life and take vows as a nun, Olive went ahead with her plans.

Ten years in a third rate boarding-house had given Olive more of an insight into the psychology of hotel work than any amount of professional courses. She saw the old and the lonely who could barely endure the sea winds and the bracing air and who hardly left the sun lounge during their two-week visit. She knew they came for company, and that the anticipation was much better than the holiday. She saw the couples with their children hoping that the two-weeks vacation would be a rest, a bit of peace, a time to get to know each other again, and she saw her mother disappointing them year after year by frowning at the children, complaining about noise and in general making the parents much more anxious than they would have been had they remained at home in the normal daily round. Oh, the number of times Olive would have loved to have been in charge, she knew what she would have done. She would have had a special room for the children with lino on the floor, a room where it didn't matter if they kicked the furniture or made a noise. She would have offered the guests a welcoming drink when they arrived instead of making an announcement about what time she expected them to be in.

But in the years of watching the visitors come and go, Olive gained what she thought was an insight into the returned emigrants, those who lived the greater part of their life in big English cities. What they seemed to appreciate so much when they came back was the smallness of the place, the fact that people saluted other people and knew all about them. These might have been the very things that they fled to London and Birmingham and Liverpool to avoid, but it certainly seemed to be something their souls cried out for now. Olive knew that when she had enough money she would run a place for Irish people in London, and she would make a small fortune. Not a big fortune, she didn't want that, just a little fortune. So that she could live in comfort, and could surround herself with nice furniture, nice pictures, so that she needn't worry about having two bars of the electric fire on. The kind of comfort which would mean she could have a bath twice a day, and take a taxi if it were raining.

And in her terraced house in Pimlico she built up the hotel of her dreams.

It had taken time. And a great deal of effort. For a year she lost money – heavy, frightening sums, even though she regarded it as an experiment. She advertised in local papers in boroughs where there were large Irish populations, she attracted lonely people, certainly, but not the ones she could help. Too many of her guests turned out to be working-on-the-Lump men who had forgotten their real names because they used so many in so many different jobs, men who appeared on no social welfare list, men who knew that if they got a bad dose of pneumonia or broke a leg that the other lads would pass a hat round for them, but there would be no pension, no insurance, no security.

They didn't stay long in Olive's little hotel, and she made them uneasy, asking where they were from and what they did.

'Sure the police wouldn't ask me that, Mam,' a man had replied to her once when she had asked some simple and she thought courteous question about his origins.

Then she had the con-men. The charmers, the people who were expecting money shortly, who cashed cheques, who told tales. It was an apprenticeship, she was learning. Soon she thought she was ready and she advertised again. By this time she had the hotel the way she wanted it. Not splendid, nothing overawing, but comfortable. There wasn't a hint of a boarding-house about it, no sauce bottles appeared with regularity on stained cloths. She arranged a weekly rate which included an evening meal, with no refund if the meal were not taken. She knew enough about her future clients to know that they were the kind of people who would like to be expected home at a quarter to seven. They could always go off out again afterwards.

She implied that those she was accepting were people of good manners and high standards. This was done very cunningly and without any hint of appearing restrictive. Whereas her mother would have said: 'I want no drink brought into the bedrooms', Olive said: 'I want you to consider this house very much as your home. I know you don't want to be in the kind of place where people have bottles in bedrooms.'

She chose the guests carefully. Sometimes after several interviews where she always gave them tea and managed to explain that it was simply a matter of having promised the place to somebody else who was to let her know by Thursday. It took her a year to build up to twelve and she sat back satisfied. They were right. They were the correct mix. They depended on her utterly, they needed her, and for the first time in her life she felt fulfilled. She felt she had got what other people got from teaching or nursing or maybe the priesthood. People who needed them, a little flock. She never included marriage and children in her list of fulfilling lifestyles. She had seen too many less than satisfactory marriages to be impressed by the state. And anyway she was too busy. You didn't run the perfect hotel without a lot of work.

There had been a question of marriage two years ago. A very nice man indeed. A Scot, quiet and industrious. She had met him at a hoteliers' trade fair, when she was examining a new system of keeping coffee hot. He had told her that it didn't really work, he had tried one in his own hotel and it had been wasteful. Their friendship got to a stage where her twelve guests were rustling and ruffled like birds in a coop fearing the intrusion of an outsider. Alec came to tea so often on Sundays that there were definite fears he might either join the establishment or else spirit Olive away. The ruffled feelings were balm to Olive, the ill-disguised anxiety among those men and women who paid her hefty sums of money to live with her was almost exhilarating. Olive kept them and Alec in suspense for some weeks and finally sent Alec away confused, wallowing in the luxuriating relief and happiness of the civil servants, bank clerks, book keepers, shop assistants and bus driver who were now her family.

She finished her list of entries in the ring file with the information that Judy O'Connor, the nice girl who worked in the chemist shop, had a brother who was a missionary and that he was coming back from Africa and through London on his way home to Ireland for Christmas. Olive thought it might be a nice occasion to have a Mass in the hotel.

Well, why not? They were all Irish, they were all Catholic. Even the three little Spaniards, José, his wife Carmen and her sister Maria, they were Catholics, they would love a Mass in the dining-room. It would make it all much more like home. She must start putting it in Judy's mind soon. Olive was careful for people not to think that all the good ideas came from her. She let the guests think that it was their idea to strip their own beds on Monday mornings and leave all the dirty linen neatly ready for the laundrymen. The guests thought that they had suggested pooling fifty pence a week each to have wine with Sunday lunch.

Hugh O'Connor was absolutely certain that *he* had broken off his engagement to that rather forward hussy who had no morals and wanted to come in and share his room saying that it was perfectly all right since they were engaged. Annie never realized that it was Olive who suggested she should break her ties with Mayo, she thought she had done it herself. The guests thought that it had just come about that they all stayed in the hotel for Christmas, they saw nothing odd about it. Olive had carefully managed to distance herself from those who had been rash enough to go to relations or friends. They had felt lacking in some kind of spirit and had felt deeply jealous when they returned afterwards to hear about the wonderful turkey, and the presents and the carols by the Christmas tree and the Pope's Blessing in the morning and the Queen's speech in the afternoon – a combination of what was best about both cultures.

The last thing that Olive did on her List day was to write home. Her father was in hospital now, her mother almost crippled with arthritis. She sent them regular small contributions with pleasant cheering letters. She had no intention of returning home. They were nothing to her now. She had a real family, a family that needed her.

Vauxhall

On the first Sunday of the month Andrew's parents came to lunch. They arrived winter and summer at midday precisely ... and every single time Andrew's father would rub his hands and ask his son how he felt about a spot of fresh air. In response Andrew would rub his own hands, pretend to consider it and then nod as if finding it a satisfactory idea.

'Back around two-fifteen – that all right dear?' he would call in to the kitchen where his mother and June were oohing and ahhing over some little gift of home-made tea cakes or tray cloths, then he and his father set off, rain or shine, for a twenty-minute walk to the pub, two and a half pints and a twenty-minute walk back home. Twelve times a year for fifteen years. That was thirty pints a year, a total of four hundred and fifty pints, but little communication shared with his father in the crowded pub which was always filled with jaded young people recovering from last night's swinging south-of-the-river party.

Then, looking at their watches anxiously in mock fear of great punishment, they left carefully at the time when last orders were being shouted and others were begging for that final injection to see them through the Sunday afternoon in Vauxhall. Andrew and his father walked back, more expansive about the roses in people's gardens, the value of property and the increase in hooliganism. When they let themselves into the flat, June and her mother-in-law would give little cries of mock relief, that the men hadn't disappeared for ever, that the lunch had not been spoiled and that they could all now sit down and have Sunday lunch.

At this point June or Andrew would go nervously to Cora's door and tap gently.

'Time for lunch, darling, Gran and Gramps are here.'

There was always a rising note at the end of the statement, questioning. It was as if they didn't know whether or not she would emerge. But she always did. Cora, their only daughter. Cora their tall fourteen-year-old only child.

The years had passed so inevitably, Andrew thought to himself that particular Sunday, as he felt the familiar relief surging through him when Cora came out, her long hair neatly held with a blue ribbon, her soft navy sweater coming well down over her jeans so that it actually looked some kind of formal attire. A huge smile for both grandparents, a kiss, an exclamation of pleasure over the joint – it was always lamb, beef or pork on a first Sunday but since Cora had been old enough to exclaim she had done so. Andrew looked at her with his constant bewilderment. How had he and June produced this lovely, blonde, distant creature? What went on in her head? What did she think of him really as she sat at his table and ate a Sunday roast with his wife and his parents? Would he ever know?

This Sunday was no different to any other. Mother had a hilarious tale about some new people who had moved into their road and had decided to invite all the neighbours in for drinks. The neighbours had disapproved strongly of such over-familiarity but had accepted, and everything had gone wrong – episode after episode of disaster from burst pipes, and clogged loos and stone cold cocktail sausages, to running out of sherry, were revealed to peals of laughter from June, grunts of recollection from father and a polite attention from Cora. To Andrew it seemed suddenly a cruel, heartless tale, unlike his mother's normal generosity, but then he remembered she often told little stories of the discomfiture of others. It made her own position more satisfactory.

June followed it with stories of the Residents' Association in the block of flats, and how they had forced the landlords to do up the entrance, and forced the council to improve the street lighting, and how they had forced the family in the top floor not to cook dishes which could be smelled all over the block.

Even though they often talked about the Residents' Association Andrew thought that today the chat seemed very militant; he got a momentary vision of all those old ladies and retired bank officials who seemed to be its inner circle, dressed up with arm bands and high boots. He smiled to himself.

Father was brought into the conversation by the two chatty women – his wife and daughter-in-law didn't want to monopolize the conversation: did he think that it was worth buying a cover for those plastic bags where people grew vegetables in cities, or should they be left to breathe, or would they look nice covered with attractive stones like a mini rockery or was there a danger that this might suffocate the tomatoes? To every one of these points Father gave his usual attention. His years of being a diplomatic clerk in chambers made him unwilling to come down too firmly on any side even in something as untendentious as this. He weighed everything happily and the audience listened respectfully.

It was a wet Sunday, which meant that they would not go for the little stroll down to the Albert Embankment, or the little walk to the park. When it rained they played Scrabble, looked at gardening catalogues, or Mother sometimes read an entire letter from Andrew's sister in New Zealand, full of people that none of them knew; but Mother would speculate happily and say: 'I think Vera is the one married to the Scottish chap, the couple they went camping with.' Then at four-thirty they had tea, and at five they were in their car, thanking and explaining that they had to go, because of the light in the winter and because of the traffic in the summer. Six times a year Andrew's father said to him: 'We'd better push off so's we can get home in the light, you know.' Six times a year: 'Have to leave now, otherwise we'll get into a hell of a mess with all the traffic building up.' Over fifteen years each phrase must have been said ninety times with an air of newness and discovery, and they had all nodded sagely. Since Cora had been old enough to nod she had always looked politely disappointed that they had to leave, but understanding as well.

'They were in very good form weren't they?' said June brightly as she pushed the tea trolley to the kitchen. Cora had disappeared to her room.

'Yes,' said Andrew getting the tea-cloth.

'Oh, will you? Thank you, love,' said June, even though Andrew had wiped the dishes after one hundred and eighty lunches and afternoon teas attended by his parents. There had always been a tradition that the lunch table was cleared and stacked neatly in the kitchen, not washed up at once.

'Andrew and I enjoy doing it later,' June always said.

'Next month is birthday month,' June said cheerfully. 'We'll have to think of what to get.'

By an odd coincidence all their birthdays fell in the same month, and this year his parents would both be seventy-five, he and June would be forty-five and Cora would be fifteen.

They had always celebrated it as a big family feast, one birthday cake for everyone, lots of presents and cards; and his mother and father always brought the cards that they had received from all their friends as well, and Cora had to say which of her school friends had given her a card.

'We've only got to hold out another fifteen years, and then we can have four generations,' Andrew said thoughtfully. 'Father and Mother could well make it to ninety don't you think?'

'What on earth do you mean?' June paused in the violent scrubbing of a difficult saucepan.

'Well, they're thirty years older than us, we're thirty years older than Cora . . .'

The same pang that always struck him when Cora was mentioned hit him sharply in the chest. He knew so little about her. Was it possible that this girl would soon be loved by a man, or desired by one?

He felt a chill at the thought. It wasn't a question of thinking her too young and innocent. In fact he had been pleased rather than distressed when he had seen one of her schoolfriends, an attractive boy, with his arm across Cora's shoulder one day walking from the bus. She had been carefully instructed in the Facts of Life by June with the help of an illustrated booklet. June had said that it was far more difficult than actually giving birth to her in the labour ward. Cora had read the pieces with interest and said; 'Oh, I see, thank you very much.'

June had tried to leave the door open for more discussion but it never came from Cora. So, from time to time she tried to add little helpful hints.

'You see, there's nothing *wrong* with feeling sexually attracted to someone. In fact it's all absolutely right if you see what I mean. The problem is that we start feeling these, um, feelings when we are rather too young to do anything about them. But they're not wrong or shameful you know.'

'Oh no,' Cora had agreed. 'I didn't think they were.'

'It's just that, economically, it would be silly for boys and girls to get married to each other and what not at thirteen and fourteen because they have no wages or money for a house, you do see?'

'Oh, yes, I see, it would be ridiculous,' Cora had said.

'I think she understood,' poor June had whispered. 'But she didn't sort of react or anything, so I can't be certain.'

Andrew knew exactly what she had meant.

Of course he was quite insane to think that because he and June had followed his parents so precisely in what they had done, Cora would do the same. She might even become part of a commune with lovers all over the house, he shuddered to himself. But then he dismissed that. It could involve a jollity, an intensity too, things that didn't characterize his cool, young daughter. An attractive young teenager, almost a young woman.

'I wonder,' he said tentatively, 'I wonder whether Cora should have her own party next month? You know, teenagers, records, dancing. She might like that. After all girls of fifteen seem grown up to each other these days.'

'A party? Here?' June was not aghast, but it was something that had never occurred to her. 'Do you think she'd like that?'

'Well, teenagers do,' said Andrew. 'Don't they?'

'And she has been to other people's birthday parties I suppose,' said June.

They looked at each other across the draining rack, their faces showing not so much shock that their daughter was turning into a young woman, but total confusion about what kind of young woman she might become. Neither of them knew.

'Shall I ask her, or will you?' asked June.

'I will if you like,' Andrew replied.

They finished the wiping and tidying in silence. Later on Cora would emerge from her room around seven and they would have a light supper. This was Cora's little job. She had been doing it now for about three years. Baked eggs, or sardines on toast, or cold meat and tomatoes if there had been a lot left over from the Sunday joint. She always prepared it quietly with no complaints, and washed up after it. She had been no trouble. Ever. Andrew wondered why he was defending her to himself. Nobody had attacked her.

This Sunday it was sardines. He joined her in the

kitchen as she was cutting the crusts from the bread.

'Do you mind doing this Cora, would you prefer to be out with your friends?'

'No, of course I don't mind, Dad,' she smiled at him remote as a stranger who has done you a small service, like giving you more room in a bus or picking up a parcel you have dropped.

'Would you like your own party next month, when you're going to be fifteen?' he said straight out. 'With music and lights and beer for the boys and a kind of wine cup for the girls.'

She looked at him for a couple of seconds.

He tried to read what was on her face.

'Dad,' she began. He had never seen her at a loss before.

'Dad. No. I think I won't. It's very kind of you and Mum, but honestly.'

'But why, love? We'd like you to have a party, a real party for your friends. Perhaps it isn't beer and wine cups. You tell us, and we'll do it right.'

She looked wretched.

'Or you do it . . . you know we won't interfere, we'll be so much in the background we'll have faded into the wallpaper,' he laughed nervously.

With the knife she was using for the toast still in her hand she started to fasten up the buttons of his cardigan and unfasten them and fasten them again. She was as tall as he was, her hair fell over her face and she left it there.

'Dad, it's really very nice of you, but I've got everything I want. Honest. I don't want a party. Honestly'

She seemed to feel that his buttons were now satisfactory and she moved back to the table.

He felt more hurt than he had ever felt and it must have shown in his face.

'We'd do it right, you know,' he said childishly.

'Of course you would, but there's no right way or wrong way. It's just not on Dad.'

'Other people have parties. You go to other people's houses when their children have birthdays.'

'But it's such a waste, I mean, Dad, people do so much damage and they don't appreciate it, and the parents are always let down. Always. I don't know anyone who's had a party whose parents didn't get upset for about six months after it. I don't want it. Dad, not for you and Mum, you're not the type.'

'What type do we have to be to give parties that are good enough for your friends, Miss?' he said almost roaring with the pain of it.

'What do we have to do, hire a bloody disco on the King's Road, is that it?'

She had put down the knife, timidly she came over to him and went at his cardigan buttons again.

'I did them wrong,' she said. It took a great effort not to shy away from her, but he stood rigid, while she opened them and refastened them, the most intimate thing she had done since she was a toddler.

'It's not that I don't want my friends to meet you and Mum, that they won't think you're good enough – they won't see you, they won't know what you're like, they won't notice you. Can't you understand? I don't notice my friends' parents, I don't listen to them. I'm not thinking you're not good enough, Dad, you're too good to have your nice lounge all mucked up. You should be grateful to me, not all hurt.'

He felt numbed. His anger and hurt were gone but they hadn't been replaced by anything. Perhaps this is a breakthrough, he thought to himself. At least she acknowledges the possibility that I do have some feelings.

'Well, it's up to you, love,' he said. 'Your mother and I only want you to have what you want.'

She had arranged the sardines neatly, two on each piece of bread, head to tail, was putting the plates in to warm and turned on the grill.

'Honestly Dad, lunch here like always, you know, the cake and everything, that's what I'd like.'

'But it isn't much, Cora love, we'd like to do more for you, you know lunch with old fuddy duddies . . . a bit dull.'

'It's what people *do*, Dad, isn't it? I mean, you might want something different for you too when it's your birthday but that's not the point is it? I mean you don't go off and do what you want to do, you have a lunch and a cake here for Gramps and Gran. You always have, it's the way things *are*.'

He watched her put the sardines under the grill and start to make the coffee. Everything was ready on the tray. It was the way things were, it was what people did. He wondered what his old father might really like to do to celebrate being seventy-five.

Too old for a belly dancer, or a weekend in Paris probably. Father most possibly liked coming to the flat and having his walk, his two and a half pints, his lunch, his gifts, his doze over Scrabble, his tea and his drive home before the crowds. Andrew didn't know. Andrew didn't even know how he wanted to celebrate his own birthday. How did he want to spend the day? A slap-up lunch in a hotel? No. It would hurt June to think that she couldn't produce something as good as a hotel. Champagne on ice? No, he liked bitter. With a crowd of people his own age from the office and the golf club? No. It wasn't done in their set, he'd feel awkward. What he really liked was the family day, the feeling that it was everyone's birthday, and they had got through one more year, the five of them, with no disasters. That's what he really liked to do, or he supposed it was.

And if that was so for the man of seventy-five and the woman of seventy-five and the couple of forty-five, perhaps the young woman of fifteen felt the same. It was safe, it was the known thing.

It wasn't exciting, it wasn't imaginative but, by heavens, it was what people did. It was the way things were.

Stockwell

Mona had vomited when the news was given to her. It was the last thing she had expected would happen and she was very ashamed. She helped the doctor and his young aide to clean the carpet, brushing aside any of their cries that she leave it alone.

'I wouldn't hear of it. These things have to be done quickly. Have you any Borax? Good, and then I find a quick squirt with a soda syphon is good. I really am most frightfully sorry.'

The doctor finally got her to sit in a chair again. Gave her a glass of water, a pill and his hand.

'I didn't put it well. I probably gave you a far worse impression of the situation . . . you must excuse me, Mrs Lewis. I have been very crass.'

His hand tightened on hers and his kind brown eyes were filled with concern. Mona Lewis looked at him gratefully.

'Dr Barton, I can't thank you enough. You have been exactly what I needed in every way. You could not have been more supportive. It's not your fault that the diagnosis was so bad. You must realize that I am completely in your debt.'

The doctor took off his glasses and wiped his eyes. He looked at this handsome woman in front of him again and marvelled. He had told her that she had inoperable cancer of several glands. In response to her calm question, he said that he had been told it was a matter of months and probably not as many as six months. It was when he had added 'Before Christmas' that her stomach muscles had reacted even though her face had not.

How could he have been so heavy-handed, so thick-skinned, so leaden? Why did he have to mention Christmas to this glowing woman? Why remind her of the one most emotive date in the year and let her picture a family scene without her? He could have cut out his tongue.

But she encouraged him to talk calmly. She had talked calmly throughout their whole odd professional relationship. She had come to him four months previously saying that she was staying with friends in Stockwell and giving a local address. After her third visit, however, she explained that she really lived in a different part of London, it was just that she wanted a doctor far away from her friends, far away from people who might know her business. Mona Lewis lived in Hampstead and all her friends went to the same doctor. It wasn't that she didn't trust him, of course she did, but if what she suspected was wrong with her was indeed true, then she didn't want his pity, his sympathy, his concern, until she knew how she was going to cope with it.

It had seemed reasonable. He had referred her for all the tests, he had liked her breezy matter-of-fact ways. He had even had nice little chats with her which were rare for him to have with patients, since his was a largely immigrant practice and much of his work seemed to him to consist of trying to understand worried young Indian mothers who could not come to see him on any matter without the husband there to interpret and act as Chaperone. Mona Lewis with her light-hearted sense of mocking him was a special treat.

She had told him that her fingers were simply itching to re-pot the tired busy lizzies and ferns in his waiting-room. She had even bought him some plant food and left him a book on simple plant care which he had read

137

to please her. Even when she had gone for the biopsy she had remained cheerful. He had got her into a local hospital.

'Where do your family think you are this week?' he had asked, worried.

She had mentioned a husband and twin daughters of sixteen.

'I've told them I'm on a course.'

'Why?' he had asked gently. 'Why don't you tell your husband? He'd want to know.'

'Don't be ridiculous, Dr Barton, nobody would want to know that his wife was having a biopsy. Come now, that's not worthy of you.'

'Very well, let me put it another way. He would like to share these things with you, if they have to be undergone, he will want to be part of them.'

'I want to go through the first bit by myself,' she said. 'Later, later I'll talk to the others. Please let me do it this way.'

He hated having to give her the news, but there was no ethical way he could involve anyone else. He was, as she said, being supportive.

She finished her glass of water, examined the damp patch on the carpet and shook her head ruefully as if a favourite puppy, not herself, had made the mess.

'I am sorry again about that, Dr Barton, very shaming. Now, can I just settle up with you as usual, and then I'll leave you to the rest of your waiting room.'

She had established early on that she would like to be considered a private patient even though she always came in surgery hours, and she paid in cash. He hadn't liked the whole arrangement, and particularly as her diagnosis looked worse and worse. Today for the first time he was adamant about the money.

'Please, Mrs Lewis. Just pause and think about me as a human being, not just a doctor with a hand out for money from a private patient. I have given you distressing news today.'

She looked at him politely, her hand already on her wallet.

'Its quite bad enough for me to know that a charming and vital woman like you has a terminal disease and it is doubly hard to have to be the one who tells you this, can you please let me have the dignity of telling you and seeing you to a taxi or telephoning your husband, or calling a friend for you, without having to take your goddamn bank notes?'

She snapped her bag shut.

'Of course. And how considerate of you. I didn't pause to think. But no. I'd prefer to walk. I usually do walk around here, when I come to you. And take buses. I'd like to do that today. Please.'

As he shook her hand, and she assured him that she felt perfectly fine, he knew he was seeing her for the last time. She would not now come back to him. She didn't want to discuss remissions, radium treatment. She wanted to know nothing of drugs or palliatives. She implied that if anything were to be done, it might be done back in Hampstead.

'You have been exceptionally good to me. I know that professional people hate things to be irregular, and you have been wonderful at hiding your irritation that I didn't go through the more conventional channels.'

The doctor didn't know why he said it but it was uppermost in his mind so it just came out.

'People often try to ... you know ... beat it, get there first. It's not a good idea. They bungle it, and even if they don't ... well ... you know, nature does it in its own rotten way. It would be a pity to take your own life ...'

'Oh no,' she smiled at him. 'No, I agree it would be a mess. Anyway, why would I go to all these measures to find out, if I were going to do something so feeble as take a bottle of pills and a bottle of vodka?'

'I'll keep feeding those plants in case you come back

to see me,' he grinned taking his tone from hers. She liked that.

'Of course I'll come back to see you,' she smiled. 'One day when you least expect it, when all the shoots need to be trimmed.'

He watched until she had turned the corner, then he pressed his buzzer and saw a malingering workman who claimed he had a bad back, and barked at him so fiercely that the man left in terror demanding to know when Dr Barton's relief doctor would be on duty.

Mona felt dangerously calm. It was a sunny July afternoon, and everything looked quite normal. Like it often looked in this strange part of London, less planted, less cared for than her own neighbourhood. Funny that she liked it so much. She was certain that Jerry would like it too, but it was something she would never share with him. What she had to do now was go through the whole sham of tests again. It seemed silly and wasteful, but this was how she had planned it. Tomorrow, tell Jerry that she felt below par, fix an immediate appointment with Franz, allow Franz to send her for tests at the clinic, follow through, slowly and remorselessly everything she had just done.

And at every step of the way now she could be clear-sighted and calm because there was going to be nothing hanging in the balance, no doubts, no waiting to know. Because she now knew the very worst she could behave with her customary calm. Reassuring everyone, allowing no panic, being utterly fatalistic. She even had a little sentence ready. 'Don't be silly, darling, it's not a question of knowing that I'm going to die, after all we all know we are going to. I just know *when* I'm going to die. That gives me the advantage over all of you.'

She was going to be perfectly frank with the girls also. There was no hiding and whispering and pretending as there had been when her own mother had died. Six months of confusion, and hope and counter hope, and bewilderment. Mona was going to be authoritative in death as she had been in everything in life. It was sad, it was obviously very regrettable since she was only forty-six. But to look on the bright side, she had had an excellent life, she would leave behind not a dependent, unsupported family, but a husband whose every comfort had been catered for, whose house ran smoothly and easily, two attractive sixteen-year-olds who had always been able to discuss their future plans with their mother and who would not cease to do so now. She would redouble her efforts to get Marigold into art school, and to direct Annabelle towards a career in social work. She would see that they both had advisors, separate ones, and contacts. She would also establish a proper social life for Jerry so that he wouldn't be left high and dry. If only she could persuade him to learn bridge. He had withstood it so long, and yet as a widower it would be his instant passport to people's houses. Nobody would say, we must have poor Jerry around, poor chap is utterly broken up since Mona's death, instead they would think more positively and say: 'We need a fourth for bridge. How about Jerry?'

Mona hated the thought of telling Sally, her dearest friend. Sally was so utterly sentimental and emotional, she could ruin everything by arriving around at their house with flowers and autumn bouquets saying that she wanted Mona to see one more bunch of dahlias or a last autumn crocus.

She had several plans also for the school where she taught. She would explain to the principal that a new teacher must be found for the autumn term, but she would ask if she could stay on as an advisor for the first two months or so, or until her strength gave out. She also felt she should like permission to discuss some aspects of death and facing it with the older girls, since they were unlikely to have the chance again of meeting someone who was going to face it as calmly as Mona was about to do.

And as for dear Jerry, she was going to try to explain

to him how essential it was that he should marry again, lest he become eccentric and absent-minded and his whole lovely antique business fall apart. If she could find the right words to explain that posthumous jealousy cannot exist. She would be in a great sleep and nothing could hurt her or touch her. Mona realized that not everyone else felt as peaceful about facing death as she did, and she wondered whether she should give talks on the subject on the radio or to women's groups.

Thinking of women's groups reminded her of old Vera North, her mother's friend of many years, now bedridden and in a wheelchair. Mona usually went to see her once a month, but with all the tests and waiting and examinations she hadn't seen Vera for some time. I'll go today, she thought. It will give everyone an explanation of why I was out all day, and should my face look a bit gloomy in spite of myself then they'll think it was because of seeing Vera.

Vera called for tea, she had a faithful slave who had looked after her since childhood. Mona always admired the set up, they needed each other, Vera and the old retainer Annie. She didn't think it was shameful to have a maid, not if you were Vera, not if you were kind and considerate, and paid Annie a just wage.

'I've been busy,' she explained to Vera.

'I know,' Vera said. 'You look more cheerful now. You looked worried when I saw you last. Were you having a medical examination?'

'How on earth did you know?' asked Mona amazed.

'Is it a hysterectomy?' asked Vera.

'No, lymph glands,' said Mona before she realized.

'Poor Mona, you are so young, yet so courageous.' Vera did not look put out.

'I am brave, but by other people's standards, not my own. I just feel that we should take the mythology out of cancer. I mean, people are afraid to mention its name. They call it silly names, they won't acknowledge it. Such huge strides have been made in, say, attitudes

142

to mental illness, it seems strange that we cannot admit to cells going rogue which is all that cancer is.'

'I know, Mona,' said Vera gravely.

'So as a last gesture, as some kind of, I don't know, some kind of statement I suppose – I'm going to talk about it, I'm going to make it normal. Acceptable even.'

She smiled triumphantly at Vera. She just got a steady glance in return.

'You see since I *am* going to be gone by Christmas at least I know that there's some end to my courage, some defined end. It's not going to be all that hard . . . and it will make it so much easier for everyone else.'

'Do you think it will make it easier for other people?' Vera asked mildly.

'Well it stands to reason . . . if they see that I'm not terror stricken, if they see that if the one who has the bloody disease can accept it, then they will too. It will save so much time, it will cut through all that pretence, we needn't make all those absurd plans for holidays next year, when everyone knows that I won't be around next year . . .'

She was rather put out by Vera's refusal to be impressed, her unwillingness to admire such amazing bravery.

'They'll prefer to pretend. And they will definitely prefer you to pretend,' Vera said firmly.

'But that's nonsense. I'm doing it for them, I'm not going to have them go through what we went through with Mother. Vera, you must remember that, how dreadful it was.' Vera sat very still.

'How old were you when Clare died . . . seventeen, eighteen?'

'I was eighteen, Vera, and I won't put my family through such an experience. We were constantly going to the Church and lighting candles in front of statues so that Mother's illness should turn out not to be serious. The word Cancer was simply not allowed to be mentioned, there was no honesty. All the things I would like to have said to my mother but never did because we were prevented from admitting it was goodbye by some confused code of keeping quiet. If mother even knew she was dying, which I doubt, none of us had a chance to ask her if she had any last things to discuss.'

'Oh she knew,' said Vera. 'She knew very well.'

'Did she talk to you about it?' Mona was startled.

'She began by wanting to talk to everyone, you are so like her it's uncanny. She wanted to face it . . . do all the things you want to do.'

'But *why* did she not do that?'

'It caused too much pain. Simply that,' Vera said. 'She saw after a couple of days that people couldn't take it. Your father for one: "Clare, stop this, there is hope, nothing is definite. I won't have you speaking as if you are a condemned woman".'

'And other people?'

'Just the same. Me too. I wouldn't look her the eye and discuss the fact that her body was rotting, no, even though she wanted to laugh and tell me that it was nothing special, mine would rot too. I wanted to believe there was hope. I wanted not to see her getting thinner and comment that the disease was taking its toll. I wanted to say, "Yes you have lost a lot of weight and it does suit you". You see Mona, you're going to find the same thing. I know what I'm talking about.'

'But that was nearly thirty years ago,' Mona pleaded. 'Things have changed now. They must have.'

Vera touched her gently. 'Go and see if you like, and if they haven't changed, come back and talk to me.'

Mona looked at her stonily.

'I mean it, Mona, my brave young girl. Really I do. I wasn't able to do it for your mother, and I don't want to do it for you. But if I couldn't face one generation being brave, if I let her go to her death with hypocritical exclamations of how well she looked, I won't do it a second time.'

144

Mona smiled at her and stood up to go.

'I mean it,' Vera said. 'Come back any time. And think before you bare it all to the others. You and your mother are unusual in this world, the rest of us aren't so strong.'

Mona kissed her goodbye. The first time she had done that.

'And I'll tell you more about Clare too . . . you'll like her,' said Vera.

'I'll come back anyway,' Mona said. 'You don't have to bribe me. And Vera, I'll try and tell the others, it would be very good if someone made a stand. Wouldn't it?'

'Clare wanted me to marry your father,' said Vera.

'I wish you had,' said Mona.

'Perhaps I'll marry Jerry instead,' said Vera with a tinny little laugh.

And Mona left quickly before she saw the tears that were going to come from it.

Brixton

The woman in personnel was about fifty and had a silly perm, all grey bubbles like an ageing Harpo Marx. Sandy looked at her without much hope.

'Well, of course, I can try and fix you with hostels or shelters or organization addresses, Miss Ring. But quite frankly I feel sure you would do better just to find accommodation for yourself.'

'How can I do that?' Sandy asked. It was so very different to the hospital where she had trained. There, the rules about where nurses had to live were still strictly enforced. There had been a list of approved lodgings and apartments, and only in these were the nurses permitted to stay.

'The nurses seem to play musical chairs with each other,' said the Harpo Marx personnel officer disapprovingly. 'You'll be very unlucky not to see about a dozen tattered notices on the board downstairs offering accommodation.'

'That sounds great,' Sandy said eagerly. 'And if I share with someone who works in the hospital, then I'll learn the ropes a bit more quickly.'

She got a watery and unenthusiastic smile. The personnel officer obviously found as little satisfaction in her job as she had found success with her hairdresser.

There were eight notices offering accommodation. Four were too expensive, two specified that the applicant must speak Spanish. That left two. One of them had a phone number, so Sandy dialled it at once. In her

hand she had her *A to Z* so that she could identify
where the place was.

'It's SW9,' the girl said.

'Clapham?' asked Sandy studying her map intently.

'More east of it,' the girl said.

'Near the tube?'

'Yeah, four minutes.'

'How many of you in the flat?'

'Just me.'

'That's not a bad rent for a flat for two.'

'You ain't seen it, lady.'

'Shall I come over and look, and let you look at me?'

'Sure. Come now I'll make you tea.'

'That's very nice, I'm Sandy Ring.'

'That's funny. I'm Wilma Ring.'

'Hey, we might be cousins.'

'Yeah. Are you black?'

'Err . . . um . . . no. Are you?'

'Yeah, we most likely ain't cousins. See you for tea.'

It was certainly shabby, though nothing that paint
and a new hall door could not have cured, Sandy
thought to herself, but the street didn't have too much
smart paint and new hall doors. There were three bicy-
cles in the hall and a lot of very loud music came up
from the basement.

What the hell, Sandy thought, I'm not going to be on
nights for the first six months, and if I can't sleep after a
day's hospital work because of a few bars of music I
must be in bad shape. Wilma was standing at the door.

'Come in, cousin,' she called with a laugh. 'Have
some nice English tea to get you over the culture shock
of a walk through the Brixton West Indies.'

It was agreed in ten minutes. The room, the rent, the
lifestyle.

'I don't have friends in, because I'm studying, see,'
Wilma said. 'But I study in my own bedroom, so you
can have people in so long as they don't shout through
the walls. And if your guys don't eat all the food in the

fridge and take all the hot water, they can stay all night.'

'What are you studying?' Sandy wanted to know. She didn't feel like telling Wilma yet that there would be no guys for a long time, not after the guy in Wales, the one she was running away from.

'Open University. I am reading for a university degree,' said Wilma. 'When you come back tonight, remember to get yourself a lamp and bulb for your room, there's only a centre light, it makes it even worse than it need be.'

'I can come back tonight?' Sandy said.

'I can't see why you should pay a hotel and pay me. You've only got one body and it can only sleep in one bed.'

For a few weeks they rarely saw each other. Wilma worked strange hours on the admission shifts, so that she could have appropriate time off for her studying and to watch the programmes on television. Sandy worked a day shift on the neuro-surgical ward. It was demanding and sometimes depressing. She often wished that Wilma were there to chat to when she got back. Bit by bit she got used to the area; they even joked with her in the corner store as she refused ackee and salt fish and other Jamaican treats.

'I only like the patties,' she said firmly.

'You wait till you go out to the island and have goat curry,' Nelson, the good-looking man who ran the shop, used to say to her. 'Then you never eat anything else.'

'I can't imagine going to Jamaica,' she said truthfully. 'It must be such a contrast between the rich tourists and the poverty of the people who live there.'

'What makes you think that?' Nelson wanted to know.

Sandy was about to say that if so many Jamaicans came to Britain to live in what she considered relative poverty, things must be in a very bad state back home.

148

But she was unsure if that would be offensive, so instead she muttered vaguely about something she had seen on television.

'You don't take no notice of that Wilma,' Nelson had said. 'Wilma is a no-good communist, she is always finding something wrong with every society.'

The day she heard this new slant on her flat-mate, Sandy climbed the stairs and found Wilma at home. She had washed her hair and was sitting in an unaccustomed relaxed mood with her feet on the window box, a towel around her head and a beer in her hand.

'Come on, pretend we're in the sun-soaked Caribbean. There's a beer for you in the fridge,' she called to Sandy and they sat in the summer evening listening to the sounds from the street below, the planes overhead, the distant traffic, and the general hum of city noises.

'I hear you're a communist,' Sandy said lightly.

'That pretty boy Nelson has a big mouth an' no brain,' commented Wilma, unperturbed.

'I think he fancies you. He always mentions you,' probed Sandy.

'Yeah, he should fancy Margaret, the mother of his three children. She works sixteen hours a day for him. He should discuss her politics and her tits, not mine,' retorted Wilma, this time with more spirit.

'But *are* you a communist?' persisted Sandy. In a way she hoped Wilma was. It was quite outrageous enough to share with a Jamaican woman, that had them all whispering back in Wales, but a Jamaican communist, would be over the top.

'Of course not, dope,' said Wilma. 'Would I be lying here talking chicken shit to a silly little nurse like you, drinking beer, if I were a communist? No, I would be fighting the good fight somewhere and overturning things. Not planning to become rich and middle class and have a university degree.'

'I think you are mad to try and do all that studying,' said Sandy, stretching her tired muscles. 'It's bad

149

enough doing what we do. I only want to sleep and look at telly when the day is over. Study! I couldn't even think of it.'

'I had always heard they were ambitious in Wales,' Wilma said.

'They may be. I'm not any more. Anyway, being a nurse isn't that far below being a teacher, you know, they rate about the same. And teachers don't get all that much more money. I don't know why you're killing yourself if all you'll do is teach in the end.'

'I'll do both,' said Wilma.

'How can you do both?' Sandy became suddenly irritated at the calm way this tall girl had everything planned. Even her short burst of leisure was carefully planned, hair shampooed, fresh air by the window, lounging in a robe, instead of sitting there, tired and hot, like Sandy was.

'I'll be a teacher during the day, and then some nights a week I'll do a night shift, and I can work full-time nursing in the long holidays. Teachers have vacations of three to four months, you know, when you add it all up. It is a ridiculous life . . . they get paid . . . I don't know.' She shook her turbanned head from side to side in amazement.

'My sister married a teacher in Wales. They don't get well paid I tell you, and he's knackered come the summer when the exams are over. You've got it wrong,' Sandy said. She didn't like to hear of people doing two jobs. She felt quite proud of herself, having managed to drag herself unwillingly from Wales, from a man who walked on her, to a big strange city and find a job and a flat. She thought that Wilma was pushing it.

Wilma got them more beer.

'Ohh,' she sighed. 'Ohh, Sandy girl, if only you knew what my mother had to do for me, and what she and her sisters have had to do for all our family. I'll *never* stop getting degrees, every letter I have to my name is a shaft of sunlight for them. It's a reason to go on scrubbing floors, to go into offices and shops at five a.m. where the air is stale and the baskets are full of yesterday's sour milk cartons, but the letters after my name will make it worth while.'

'Oh, for heaven's sake, Wilma, you're far too intelligent to go along with that crap,' cried Sandy, annoyed now and tactful no longer. 'If you really wanted to help your mother, then you'd give her money, for God's sake. I mean, I send my mother money each week, not much, but a little, for her to get herself something nice, maybe a hair-do or a night at the bingo and a fish supper. My Dad keeps her very short.'

'Oh yes?' said Wilma.

'Yes, bloody yes. And that's what you should do instead of filling your poor Mam's head up with ideas and nonsense, and degrees and airy-fairy letters after your name. If you can't bear her being down on her knees then take her off them. You can send her ten quid a week – better, you can go and give it to her. She only lives an hour away. I can't understand why you don't go to see her more. My Mam lives hundreds of miles away, otherwise I'd go and take her out on a Saturday night for a bit of a laugh. That's what a daughter is for.'

Wilma sat up and looked at her.

'No, Sandy my little sister, that is *not* what a daughter is for. A daughter must never be for that. That means the system never ends. A daughter must be something better, something stronger, she must give hope and reason for what is being done. She must make some sense out of all the scrubbing, bring some logic to all that lavatory cleaning. Otherwise a daughter is just yourself again, on and on for ever.'

Sandy saw why Nelson thought that Wilma wanted to overturn society.

And because she thought of Nelson she mentioned him.

'But the other Jamaicans don't feel that way, Nelson

151

and those girls in the store for example, they have a laugh and they go to parties and they sing songs, and they say it's not too bad. Isn't that better for a mother, to see she has happy children?'

Wilma stood up and rested her hands on the window box. She looked as if she were about to make a speech to a crowd below but instead she spoke in a very gentle voice.

'My mother told me that before she came here she never knew that white women were poor too, when she saw poor white women in Britain she thought they had done something bad and were being punished. She came from a family where the women were strong.

'*Her* mother remembered being a Mammy and remembered having to lie down and let a white boss screw her. But that had all gone by my mother's time, she had five jobs, five different jobs to get her fare to England, and when she came here she had six jobs to make the money for us to come, but she didn't mind having six jobs because she lived in luxury. She had electricity, not kerosene, she had water in a tap, down the corridor but in a tap. She had a house where the food didn't melt, or rot, or go bad, she didn't have to buy expensive ice to keep food fresh for twenty-four hours. And one by one she sent for us. One by one we came.'

Her voice began to sound a little like a preacher's. Sandy could imagine her putting a few 'Yea, verrilys' into her conversation.

'You see, what was so wonderful was that we knew she would send for us. I was only nine when she went, only a child of nine when she got on the bus to Kingston that day, and I knew she would send for us one by one. That when I came first, part of her sending for Sadie and sending for Margaret and the others was that I should work hard at school. It was team work, it was solidarity like you've never known. If we had the homework done and our Mother's supper ready when she came in from one job, that gave her strength to go out to another. If she didn't have to worry about us, if we cleaned the house, then she could stay healthy, in her jobs and not fret. You have to scrub a lot of floors and get a lot of bonus and overtime to pay five airfares from Jamaica and for a home for them to live in.'

Wilma smiled seraphically.

'But we were a lucky family because it was the woman who came. No danger of the woman finding a fancy man and forgetting us like happened to some of the men who came. A woman with five children will not forget them. That Nelson you admire so much in the corner store, he has a wife and two children in Ocho Rios, as well as Margaret and the three children here. Nice for Nelson to be chatty and to have a laugh and a drink and a song. Very nice. My mother would spit on him. A disgrace to Jamaica, every song and every bit of a laugh which you said I should be having is a mockery.'

'But, Wilma, surely you can have both. I mean the pride in your doing well *and* a bit of a laugh, that's all I was suggesting. That's all I was saying, your Mam has to have some relaxation, some happiness.'

'I write to her and I tell her what I am studying, sometimes she looks at the television when the Open University programmes are on. She can't understand them, but that's her happiness.'

'What does she do on her time off?'

'She sleeps. And when she wakes to work again she remembers that her mother couldn't read but she can read and write, and she knows that even though she can read and write she will never have qualifications but I will have a university degree, and that sends a big surge of happiness right through her and she is glad that she didn't just sit and laugh with her mother while the chickens ran around the dusty yard, and that I did not sit and laugh with her, while we both went out to play bingo.'

'I see,' said Sandy, who didn't see at all.

'You don't see, because for you it has always been a possibility, a good life. You don't have to prove anything to your mother nor she to hers.'

'Oh I don't know. I've had more education, a better job, more freedom than she did.' Sandy didn't want anyone to think that there had been no progress. Life hadn't been a bed of roses in the small Welsh town.

Wilma sighed. Sandy was by far the nicest of the girls who had shared her flat, but she would leave, she would leave soon. Without a proper explanation. And Nelson would say that she left because she was too toffee-nosed for the area, and Old Johnny, the man from Barbados two floors down, would say that it was good riddance to that young whitey anyway, and only Wilma would know that it had nothing to do with colours of skin or area, or smells of curry or steel bands in the basement. It had everything to do with life being short and most people wanting to have a laugh and a good time.